The Case Of Stolen Time

Book One

The Case Of Stolen Time

The Misadventures Of Inspector Moustachio

by Wayne Madsen

illustrated by Lisa Falzon

PUBLISHED BY

Community
PRESS

VIRGINIA BEACH, VIRGINIA

Published By
COMMUNITY PRESS
239 Windbrooke Lane
Virginia Beach, VA 23462

Library Of Congress Control Number: 2006939900
ISBN 978-0-9790878-9-9

Printed In The United States Of America
12 11 10 09 08 07   10 9 8 7 6 5 4 3 2 1

2007 First Edition

Visit our website at www.communitypresshome.com

This book is dedicated to my wife Beth and my children Jake and Alexa for giving me — every day— the power to believe.

To Jake W. Madsen, for the ingenious creation of the character of Inspector Moustachio.

To Alexa V. Madsen, for the brilliant and beautiful inspiration for Inspector Girl.

To Grandma Cacossa, for the mysterious quirkiness that is Grandma Moustachio.

And to Rex the Cat for being Rex the Cat.

Contents

chapter
one
The Magnifying Glass

"Grandma Moustachio's here, Jake!" exclaimed Alexa as she pressed her nose up against the frosty glass of her bedroom window.

Jake and Alexa had been waiting very patiently for their Grandmother to arrive. It was Jake's eleventh birthday, and his Grandma had promised him a fantastic surprise when she came over to baby-sit that evening.

Jake had a huge smile on his face as he yelled through the hallways., "I can't wait to open my birthday present."

"I wonder what it is?" said Alexa as she met him outside the playroom, which was filled with gifts galore from Jake's birthday party that afternoon.

"I don't know," he said with a big grin.

Alexa reached up on her tippy toes and grabbed her favorite doll off the top toy shelf. Her doll had the same big blue eyes and long strawberry blonde hair as she had. "I hope it's another U.S.A. Girl Doll," she said.

"A doll," moaned Jake. "Dolls are for eight-year-old girls. I'm expecting something big! Bigger than big, BIG! BIG!"

Large, fluffy snowflakes started to sprinkle down to the

ground outside the Moustachio's home. As the backdoor opened up, a blast of frigid air from the January sky poured into the warm toasty house. The children raced each other franticly through the house, sliding on the shiny wood floor to see who could reach Grandma first.

"I'm here!" shouted Grandma.

"Grandma, Grandma, you're here!" screamed Alexa as she grabbed her hand and tugged her grandmother further into the house. "Come quickly into the playroom so we can open up Jake's present."

Grandma Moustachio scurried up into the playroom, brushing snowflakes out of her wild and crazy, salt and pepper hair. Alexa walked behind her, picking up hair pins as they fell out of her grandmother's hair. She placed half of them neatly in her own hair as she created a new hairdo. With the remaining hair pins Alexa made a matching hairstyle for her U.S.A. Girl Doll and then placed her back on the toy shelf.

"What's this?" Grandma asked, looking at the floor as she plopped down on the large, overstuffed, flowered sofa.

The children were just finishing up a game of House Detective that they had started earlier. Jake and Alexa dove to the game board where scorecards were spread all over the playroom floor.

"We're playing House Detective, Grandma," Jake said as he looked patiently at Alexa, whose turn it was to guess the culprit of the crime.

Alexa raised her left eyebrow and did a final check of her scorecard. She smirked at Jake, almost assured of a correct guess. "It was Mrs. Pumpernickel, in the garden, with the candlestick."

"You win!" frowned Jake, as he scratched his head.

"I have a birthday present for my favorite, red-headed, eleven-year-old boy!" Grandma exclaimed. "Why, I think you get taller every time I see you."

"I'm the tallest boy in my class," he said, stretching himself taller as he stood up.

Grandma proceeded to open up her very large, black, canvas pocket book, which was always filled with many wonderful and mysterious treasures.

Bouncing from sofa to sofa, Jake yelled, "Show me! Show me!" His big, green eyes opened as wide as they could go in anticipation of what she had buried deep beneath the clutter of her pocketbook.

At that moment, she pulled out the most wonderful magnifying glass the children had ever seen. The round glass sparkled like a shooting star and was surrounded by a golden frame with a cherry wood handle.

"This was your Grandpa's most cherished possession," she said as she fumbled for her crossword puzzle. "It always brought him such luck on all of his cases when he was a detective for the police department."

"Wow!" exclaimed the children.

Jake snatched up the magnifying glass and immediately started to bounce around the room, inspecting the wrinkles on his Grandmother's face.

She looked somewhat amused and a little annoyed as he moved the magnifying glass all around her face. "Hey, not so close," she muttered. "This magnifying glass is now yours, Inspector Moustachio!"

"Cool, Grandma, I can use this on all my adventures!" he exclaimed.

The children's dad came down the stairs all dressed up in his blue suit and his favorite yellow tie with the blue stripes on it. "You mean misadventures," said Dad as he adjusted his tie.

The children's parents were on their way to a party. Mom was still upstairs fussing over her last minute bedtime preparations for the children. She placed Alexa's purple, satin U.S.A. Girl pajamas on the corner of her white princess bed and then grabbed Jake's green and brown camouflage PJ's and tossed them on the top of his blue, roaring-race-car-shaped bed.

"Lexy and Jake, did you brush your teeth yet?" yelled Mom from above.

"We sure did!" exclaimed Alexa.

"I put your pajamas on your beds," she said as she walked down the stairs in a beautiful, pink, fuzzy sweater and skirt with shoes so high Jake thought she might topple over. Still trying to get her last sparkly earring in her right ear, she said, "Be in bed in one hour and don't get into too much mischief."

"The children and I will have loads of fun!" said Grandma.

"Bye, Mom! Bye, Dad! We love you!" shouted the children.

"Love you, too," said Mom as she grabbed her overstuffed white coat that reminded the children of a large polar bear.

Dad grabbed his coat and car keys and yelled from the closet door, "Don't forget to feed the cat."

"We won't," said Jake as he cleverly slid the House

Detective game under the sofa so he wouldn't have to clean it up.

Mom and Dad hurried out the back door into the frosty night. Jake and Alexa were filled with excitement about what to look for next with the magnifying glass.

"Why don't we search for the cat?" asked Alexa.

"That's a marvelous idea," said Grandma as she pulled a pencil out of her fluffy hair. "I will start my crossword puzzle, and you look for your furry pal, Rex, until bedtime."

"We'll have ourselves a short adventure!" declared Jake.

"I'll grab my Inspector Girl backpack in case we need any supplies," said Alexa.

chapter two
The Attic

Alexa ran upstairs to her overly-pink bedroom with the numerous stuffed animals scattered across her bed and charged straight for the closet. She pulled everything out until she found her pink and purple Inspector Girl backpack that Grandma had given her for her sixth birthday.

Jake and Alexa then proceeded to comb the house for any clues of Rex, their rusty-colored, furry pal. The children found many interesting things while looking through the magnifying glass: a small piece of popcorn behind the sofa, a hair pin that fell from Grandma's hair onto the kitchen floor, an old sock of Dad's behind the coffee table, but no sign of Rex!

"Where do you think that pesky cat is?" questioned Jake, curious as he leaned over to examine the crack in Mom's vase that he had crazy glued yesterday after his airplane had accidentally flown into it.

"I think he's hiding in the attic," Alexa whispered. "And Mommy knows *all* about that crack!"

"Lexy!" he scolded. "Did you tell?"

Alexa tossed her hair back and exclaimed, "I didn't have to; you glued the flower upside-down."

Jake and Alexa slowly tip-toed up the attic stairs, examining each step with the magnifying glass as they got closer and closer to the door. Jake turned the door knob with some hesitation. It squeaked open. Jake poked his head in first, with Alexa squeezing right in behind him.

"Do you see anything, Jake?" she asked as she sniffed the musty smelling air.

"Too dark," whispered Jake.

They entered the room cautiously as Jake found the light switch. The attic was dusty and smelled of old things from years gone by.

"Look, Lexy, here's your old rocking horse," said Jake, jumping into the saddle. Jake began to rock back and forth as Alexa put on her old cowgirl vest. She threw her old, red, cowgirl hat with the white fringe on top of Jake's head.

"Giddy up, horsy!" he yelled. "Giddy up!"

Alexa laughed so loud she nearly tore the stitching off the tiny pink and red vest. As she pulled off the vest, she sighed, "I can't believe I was ever that small."

"Hmmmm . . . those were the good old days, huh Lex," said Jake, jumping off the horse.

"Most definitely, Inspector!" agreed Alexa.

Suddenly, a huge green and red box filled with Christmas ornaments started to fall from a top shelf. Silver and gold tinsel showered from above. The box hit the light switch off before crashing to the floor.

"REX!" shouted the children.

"Quick, Jake, grab the flashlight and the magnifying glass!" Alexa exclaimed. "It's time for us to put our detective skills to work!"

The children ran around wildly in the dark, squealing with delight as they hunted for their absent cat. The tinsel was flying everywhere as they heard Rex running around the attic jumping from box to box. Rex knocked over everything in his path, including an old box of blankets that fell over the children's heads.

"Can you see him, Jake?" shouted Alexa. "Can you see him?"

"I can't see anything with this old baby blanket on my head," said Jake, "but I think he is tapping on the magnifying glass."

Jake proceeded to pull the blanket off his head so he could get a better look into the magnifying glass. His red hair was sticking straight up from the static electricity that radiated from the blanket.

"Cool!" he said as he looked closer and closer with the flashlight into the magnifying glass. "Look how BIG Rex's eyeball is!"

Alexa became scared and started to shake and stutter. She tugged on the end of Jake's red and white baseball shirt.

"JAKE — JAKE!" she stuttered.

"Lex, don't bother me," he snapped as he tried to push her out of his way. "I'm investigating Rex's eyeball."

"But, Jake!" quivered Alexa, "REX IS SITTING NEXT TO ME!"

Rex walked around Alexa and started to sniff Jake's back. Jake began to tremble when he felt Rex behind him. Then, he realized that the eyeball in the magnifying glass did not belong to his cat, after all. Horrified, both children jumped up. Their eyeballs grew as big as the one in the magnifying glass.

"Ahhhhhhhh!" they screamed.

"Run, Lexy! Run! Run for your life!" shouted Jake.

Both the magnifying glass and the flashlight went flying into the air. The cat's fur blew up like an overstuffed jelly doughnut as he MEOOOOWED in terror.

Jake and Alexa went running into the dark toward the door. Just as the children reached it, they heard a loud *BANG* as the magnifying glass and the flashlight hit the floor.

As her curiosity got the best of her, Alexa bravely clicked on the light switch to see what had happened. Rex was so scared he was sitting on top of Jake's head. The children turned to get a better look and saw in amazement the magnifying glass bouncing, shaking, and dancing on the big, knotty attic wood floor.

"Do you hear that tapping again, Alexa?" whispered Jake as he shook off his furry cat hat.

"I think it's coming from the magnifying glass! It's alive!" she whispered back.

"Don't be ridiculous. It's an inanimate object," he said. "It can't be alive!"

Jake and Alexa slowly started creeping towards the magnifying glass. As they got closer and closer, the strange tapping sound from the bouncing object got louder and louder.

"Hello! Hello! Anyone out there?" called the magnifying glass.

"Inspector Moustachio, is that you?" said the strange

voice from beyond.

Jake's hand was shaking as he picked up the magnifying glass from the floor. He looked into it with wide open eyes and, to his surprise, saw a strange little man looking back at him from the other side.

"Are you The Great Inspector Moustachio?" the little man questioned.

Jake raised his left eyebrow as he thought about an answer. His last name was, after all, Moustachio, and he truly was a great detective. "*THAT'S ME!*" he shouted. "I'm Inspector Jake Moustachio!"

"Thank heavens I found you," said the strange little man. "I desperately need your help!"

Alexa stomped over and plucked the magnifying glass right out of Jake's hand. She stuck her nose so tight against it that her long eyelashes curled around the corners of the gold frame.

"*HELP WITH WHAT?*" she yelled as the glass fogged up with every breath she took.

The little man looked puzzled and annoyed as he wiped the cloudy fog away with his red and black polka dot handkerchief. "And who are you, little lady?" he asked.

"I am Alexa Moustachio, assistant to The Great Inspector Jake Moustachio — my brother," she said. "By the way, who are you?"

"Why, I am Delbert, The Keeper of Time," he said. "I need your help, because time has been stolen!"

"*STOLEN!*" they cried.

"That's what I said," he muttered. "*STOLEN!*"

Jake and Alexa were ecstatic to finally get a real

mystery to solve. Up to now they'd been helping the little old lady up the street find out who'd been stealing her afternoon newspaper. After only one day of combing the neighborhood for clues, they'd figured out, without much excitement, it was Graham, the next door neighbor's dog, who was collecting the papers in his dog house.

Delbert stuck his eyeball up against the magnifying glass once again, and shouted, "Now, quickly, I need you on my side of the magnifying glass so you can solve this case and return time back where it belongs!"

"How do you expect us to do that?" asked Jake with a puzzled look on his face.

"You've never gone through the magnifying glass before?" he asked.

Jake scratched his head as he paced back and forth across the attic floor, kicking tinsel with his sneaker, pondering his dilemma.

"Nope!" answered Jake. "Never have."

"All you have to do," explained Delbert, "is read the words that are written on the handle of the magnifying glass three times out loud."

Jake began very carefully to inspect the cherry wood handle of the magnifying glass for the words Delbert spoke of. Jake could not see any of the words and shook his head in frustration. "I don't see anything!" he mumbled.

Alexa became annoyed and grabbed the magnifying glass out of Jake's hand to take a look herself. "I don't see anything, either!" she muttered.

Delbert looked a little worried that he might have made a mistake in calling upon Jake for help. "Look again

Inspector," he cried. "Look again. Only a truly great detective can activate the magnifying glass. I am certain that's you!"

Jake's hand trembled as he held the handle and looked again. All of a sudden a small flicker of light glimmered as the words, one by one, appeared on the handle.

Through the magnifying glass you will see,
the many misadventures that can be.

The children gasped in disbelief. "How did you do that?" questioned Jake.

"I didn't, Inspector," Delbert explained. "You did."

"He did?" asked Alexa.

"Of course!" proclaimed Delbert. "The greatest gift in life is the power to believe!"

Jake and Alexa repeated the words three times out loud as they were instructed. The magnifying glass began to shake and fell out of Jake's hand. As it fell to the floor, a huge flash of light bolted out from it. The magnifying glass was growing larger and larger!

"Grab your sister's hand, Inspector," said Delbert. "The ride gets a little bumpy from this point on!"

Alexa quickly opened up her backpack and signaled Rex to jump in. She then grabbed Jake's hand, shaking in anticipation of what was coming next.

Suddenly, a large vortex of wind shot out of the magnifying glass, spinning tinsel all around the room like socks tumble drying in Mom's dryer.

"Jump in, Inspector!" yelled Delbert. "Jump in!"

Jake and Alexa hesitated a moment then grabbed each other tightly. They looked at each other with curious grins, took a deep breath, and jumped into the magnifying glass. They slid down a gigantic endless slide, twisting and turning inside the magnifying glass. With every turn they slid faster and faster as sparkles of color and flashing stars flew past their wide-opened eyes.

"Ahhhhh!" screamed the children.

"Hold on!!!!!!" yelled Delbert. "Hold on!"

Rex, being the curious cat he was, stuck his head out of the backpack to see what was going on. The force of the wind blew against his fluffy, furry face, exciting him as his meow echoed for miles and miles into the stars.

"Don't let go of me, Jake," cried Alexa with half closed eyes. "I'm scared."

Jake held onto her as tightly as he could. "I have you, Lexy," he said. "Don't worry."

"You're almost there, Inspector," screamed Delbert.

Their fast and furious journey finally came to an end when they fell out of the magnifying glass, stumbling and rolling over each other like two beach balls in a gust of wind. Then they came to an abrupt stop. The backpack went flying upside-down across the room, knocking into an old suit of armor, trapping Rex inside.

The magnifying glass let out another burst of light and shrunk back to its original size as it hit the floor. Jake grabbed the glass as he helped Alexa up; they plucked the Christmas tinsel out of their hair and off of their clothes.

The Case Of Stolen Time

Before Jake put the magnifying glass into his back pocket, he looked back into it and saw the attic, disappearing rapidly from the other side.

chapter three
The Bell Of Time

"You made it, Inspector!" said Delbert. "Welcome."

Jake and Alexa, still dizzy from the ride, looked down and saw Delbert for the first time without the glare and the fog of the magnifying glass. He was a very short, stubby, little man with a blue-gray moustache spread across his wrinkly face. Delbert was wearing a funny, blue, captain's hat with a gold ring around the rim.

Holding up his tan pants were red suspenders, covered with little shiny gold clocks that he fiddled with nervously. He paced back and forth across the dusty stone floor of the spooky dungeon that the children now appeared to be trapped in.

"Where are we?" asked Alexa as she grabbed a pink hair tie from her pants pocket and rearranged her hair into a perfect pony tail.

"This is the basement of The Grand Museum of Time in the town of Antwerp," explained Delbert. "The birthplace of modern day time."

"Hmmmm," said Jake. "In all my six years of school, adding in one year of kindergarten and subtracting two years for preschool, I've never heard of this place!"

Delbert took off his captain's hat to scratch his head and whispered, "It's a secret."

"Ohhhh!" said the children.

"Before this castle was turned into a museum, it belonged to a world famous 14th century archaeologist and philanthropist, Lord Frederic Grimthorpe. He became obsessed with building on top of this castle the first known clock in all of Europe, but he had no way to power it. He had heard of an ancient mythological Egyptian Stone of Time, which had the power to measure and store the passage of time and events throughout history. Lord Grimthorpe knew if he could find this stone he would be able not only to run his clock, but also to use its power to create and control time as we now know it. Seconds would become minutes; minutes would become hours; hours would become days; days would become weeks; weeks would become months; and months would become years."

"Did he ever find the stone?" questioned Jake.

"He sure did!" exclaimed Delbert. "On an archeological dig just outside the Egyptian town of Giza."

"What did he do with the stone when he found it?" asked Alexa.

"Well," explained Delbert, "Lord Grimthorpe knew the possession of the stone put him and his family in grave danger from anyone who knew the stone actually existed. Since the stone turned out to be made of solid gold, he decided to disguise it by melting it down and shaping it into a tiny bell no bigger than the size of a walnut. When he finally finished building The Great Clock of Grimthorpe in the clock tower above, he hid The Bell of Time in the center of the clock. Its energy has powered The Great Clock and every other clock built since. That was, until last night when the bell was stolen and time just stopped!"

"Don't worry, Delbert," Jake said. "We'll help you get it back!"

"Oh no, my backpack is gone!" cried Alexa, looking around the room.

"It has to be somewhere in this basement," Jake answered.

They all began to search the basement for Alexa's backpack and its furry stowaway, Rex.

Jake ran down a musty hallway lined by old, wooden cuckoo clocks covered with cobwebs and spiders. "Nothing over here," he shouted.

Alexa skipped down a narrow passageway filled with boxes and boxes of unused watches when she saw a pink one hanging out of a small box and put it on her wrist. As she admired it, she said, "That's beautiful!"

"What did you say?" Jake yelled from beyond.

She quickly took off the watch and threw it back into the box. "Nothing, nothing in here either," she yelled back, resuming the hunt.

Delbert scurried across the room and found the backpack stuck in a corner behind some paintings and an old suit of armor. He yelled, his voice echoing throughout the caverns of the basement, "I found your backpack, little lady. I found your backpack."

The children followed the sound of Delbert's voice. They found him standing next to a tall, mysterious, silver-colored suit of armor that had a large, blue, fluffy feather sticking out of the helmet. The suit of armor was holding a blue-crossed shield with a blue-tipped sword that reminded the children of the evil robot from their favorite space movie.

As they ran to unzip Rex from the backpack, he popped out of it and went sliding across the floor with a half-licked, red lollypop stuck on his furry tail.

"WHAT A RIDE!" he said. *"I haven't had so much fun since Graham, that dumb dog next door, chased me up and down the yard. Helloooooo! There's a fence back here, you bone head!"*

Jake and Alexa stood there with their mouths wide open, amazed that Rex was speaking to them.

"Cat got your tongue?" joked Rex. *"Do you get it? Do you get it? Ca---, Tongue! I just crack myself up!"*

"Rex, you can talk!" exclaimed Alexa as she ripped the red lollypop from his tail.

"Ouch!" he screamed *as* his big, golden eyes teared up from the pain.

Alexa stood there holding a rusty-colored, furry lollypop.

"I've always been able to talk!" he said. *"What do you think a meow is? But you've never been able to understand me!"*

Leaping here and there, Rex screamed, *"Yahoooooo!"*

"Rex being able to speak as we do must be the result of coming through the magnifying glass," deduced Jake as he watched Rex making a spectacle of himself, rolling and leaping throughout the halls of the basement.

"Well, I don't care how it happened; I'm just thrilled to be able to understand my Rexy cat!" exclaimed Alexa as she scooped him up and gave him a big, snuggly hug.

"You know—You forgot to feed me!" Rex complained. *"How about some seafood surprise?"*

"Rex, we don't have time to eat!" admonished Alexa. "We have a mysterious case to solve."

"I can't work on an empty stomach!" Rex cried. *"Listen, sister, you have to have something in that back pack of yours to eat besides that fuzzy lollipop. And, by the way, you're not thinking of eating that, are you?"*

Alexa got an annoyed look on her face as she wrapped up the fur-covered lollipop, placing it into her Inspector Girl backpack. "Yuk," she said. "Of course I'm not!"

"Well, then, throw me some tuna or a fish stick— anything—I'm starving!" Rex demanded *as* he wedged himself between her legs.

"Rex, I don't have any cat food in here," answered Alexa as she searched through her backpack. Alexa then let out a happy scream as she found something great in her backpack.

"Is it tuna? Is it tuna?" Rex shouted ecstatically.

Alexa pulled out a pink and white head band. "I'm so excited! I've been looking for this for weeks," she said as she pulled out her pony tail and changed her hair once again.

"I'm going to die of starvation. Aren't I?" moaned Rex as he collapsed on the cold, stone floor with his paws tucked under his wilting face.

"Maybe Delbert can whip us up a snack!" suggested Alexa, making the last turn of a new French twist in her hair.

"Oh, brother!" groaned Jake as he proceeded to use his

magnifying glass to start looking for clues to solve the case. He moved cautiously around the hallways and caverns of the basement, examining everything with the detail of a true world-class detective.

He noticed that the foot of the blue-feathered suit of armor was covered in white, dusty powder. Jake bent down to inspect it further. He cleaned off the powder to reveal a large, deep scratch on the armor-plating of the right foot.

Curious, Jake raised his left eyebrow as he zoomed the magnifying glass in on something he noticed on the ground, glistening beneath the suit of armor. The object was also covered in the same white powder as the foot from the suit of armor. "What's this?" he questioned as he scooped up the object.

"Why, it appears to be a set of keys," said Delbert. "I've never noticed them there before."

Jake continued to examine the keys with the magnifying glass. They made a jingling, jangling sound as he spun them around his hand, shaking the powder off for a better look. The keys looked like they came from medieval times. Years had tarnished the sterling silver that they were made from.

They had funny cuts and holes on the handles, looking nothing like any keys he had ever seen. Each of the four keys was engraved with the letter "S".

"That's strange!" said Alexa as she stuck her finger through one of the holes on the largest key. "Why would someone leave keys on the floor of the basement?"

Jake plopped the keys into Alexa's backpack for safe keeping. "Maybe someone dropped them when they took the bell that controls time," he offered.

"Or maybe those keys are marked 'S' for opening boxes of STUPID, old, dusty junk down here," joked Rex. *"Can we eat now?"*

Alexa zipped her backpack up, then threw it over her shoulder. "We'll have to hold on to them for evidence!" she declared.

"I would be delighted to find you a snack," said Delbert, adjusting the clocks on his suspenders. "There was a grand party here last night, celebrating the exhibit of Lord Grimthorpe's collection of suits of medieval armor. He possessed the rarest collection of suits in all of Europe. They are all finally here in one place for all to see.

"The Duke of Snuffles gathered them all up from the relatives of Lord Grimthorpe and brought them here for this exhibit. All five of them are scattered throughout the museum."

Delbert pointed to the blue-feathered suit of armor across the room. "That one," he declared, "is known as The Blue Knight."

"Cool!" shouted the children as they followed Delbert out of the caverns of the basement.

"I'm sure Mrs. Smythe, the cook, can find us some leftovers from the party in her kitchen," said Delbert. "She's been anxiously awaiting your arrival."

Delbert led the children to a dimly lit stairwell in the far back corner of the basement. When they began to climb the stairs, Jake looked back into the basement and noticed a blue haze of smoke gathering around the room. He rubbed his eyes in disbelief as he saw it enter the helmet of the blue-feathered suit of armor.

"Lexy," stuttered Jake, "did — did you see that!"

Alexa quickly glanced back, adjusting her backpack to get a better look. "See what?" she whispered.

Jake scratched his head and yelled, "That blue smoke. It — it just entered the helmet on the suit of armor."

"It's kind of dark in there," she said. "It's probably your imagination."

"You're probably right," he said, squinting his eyes. "It's not like there's a ghost in there!"

"It's not your imagination, Inspector," explained Delbert as he climbed the steps. "Legend has it that the spirits of The Knights of Lion Heart haunt their old suits of armor, looking for trouble!"

"The spirit of The Blue Knight, The Red Knight, The Green Knight, The Purple Knight, and The Yellow Knight get a little tired standing around in one spot when they're in their old suits of armor," explained Delbert. "They need to stretch their rusty, old legs, you know. Don't worry, they're usually harmless."

Rex was shaking as he moved through the children's legs up the stairs. "*What do you mean — usually harmless?*" he moaned.

"Things are a little strange on this side of the magnifying glass. As you will see," replied Delbert from the stairwell.

Hearing that, Rex's fur quickly puffed up to three times its normal size. Alexa and Jake took one last look into the basement and saw The Blue Knight walking off into the darkness.

Frightened, Rex kept hitting them with his overblown furry head as they moved up step-by-step on their way to the kitchen. *"Keep moving, you two!"* he said. *"Keep moving."*

"Scaredy cat!" the children exclaimed.

chapter four

The Upside-Down, Down-Side-Up, Pineapple Cake

The children made their way up the narrow, dark stairwell to the floor above. They followed Delbert down a long hallway, finally reaching their new destination. The kitchen was a huge room filled with many antiques, surrounded by magnificent, multicolored, stained glass windows reaching almost up to the sky. Copper pots and pans hung everywhere the children could see.

"Yum-m-m-m," sighed Jake and Alexa as they smelled the heavenly cakes and pastries.

There was a long banquet table just off to the side of the main cooking area that the museum used for parties when showing new works of art. At the end of the table was a cobblestone fireplace with a roaring fire to warm the January chill. The children quickly noticed a strange looking moose head mounted above the mantel of the fireplace. The moose head was covered with a brown, bristly coat of fur with two enormous antlers sticking out of its head and big, brown eyes with long thick eyelashes.

"That's Jasper!" said Delbert pointing up to the mantel. "Lord Grimthorpe caught him centuries ago on an expedition and hung him up there to keep an eye on the place."

"*Well, with The Bell of Time stolen, it looks like he wasn't a very good watch dog,*" joked Rex, sniffing the kitchen floor for a morsel of food.

"Listen, you tiny, orange fur ball, I'm not a dog. I'm a moose. It wasn't my fault that time got stolen!" Jasper grumpily snapped from above as he yawned, having been just woken from his nap. "The bell wasn't stolen from the kitchen, you know!" he bellowed. "If I was hanging around the clock tower I might have seen something, but I didn't because I'm hanging right here!"

"*Now I've seen everything,*" said Rex, "*a talking moose head!*"

"Ah, words of wisdom coming from a talking cat," sighed Jake, examining Jasper closer with his magnifying glass.

The children were giggling and smiled from ear to ear as they listened to the talking moose head arguing with their talking cat.

"And, as you can see, I'm just a mounted moose head. I don't have a body to go running around the museum with either," Jasper yelled down to Rex angrily, a gust of his stinky moose breath filling the room.

"*Wow—,*" laughed Rex, rolling around on the floor. "*Get this dude a large toothbrush and a gallon of mouthwash. He stinks!*"

Jasper crinkled his snout, exploding, "I just hang here all day long and see what I can see, when I see what I can see! You see!"

"We all see," shouted the cook, Mrs. Smythe, stepping into the kitchen from the butler's pantry. Mrs. Smythe was a large woman, wearing a brightly-colored clock apron draped over her red uniform. Her gray hair was tightly fastened into a bun perched high upon her head. She reminded Jake of the no-nonsense and very strict school cafeteria lady who never let them have any fun during lunch time. "Now, stop your belly aching, you old moose head," she yelled to Jasper. "Let the Inspector get back to work."

Mrs. Smythe looked like a gigantic, red checker as she glided across the red and black checkerboard floor to greet Jake and Alexa. "Without time working, I won't be able to properly bake my upside-down, down-side-up, pineapple cake for the town picnic's baking contest," she sternly announced.

"You know," said Jasper as he swirled his head, knocking his antlers on both sides of the fireplace, "except for last year, she's won first prize four times in the last five years. Her secret is the vanilla baking powder used to make her cake."

"What happened last year?" asked Jake, maneuvering around Mrs. Smythe with the magnifying glass, trying to look for clues.

"Mrs. Panosh, the cook from the zoo, won with her right-side, left-side, cherry, chocolate-glazed, marble pie," Mrs. Smythe said crankily as she started mashing potatoes with a large mallet on the counter top. Potato chunks went flying all over the place with each crazy swing of her mallet. "Someone put my upside-down, down-side-up, pineapple cake on the mantel right next to that smelly hairy moose.

When I got back to the kitchen, that mangy moose head had eaten all of my famous cake, leaving me but a crumb to serve. I had nothing to enter into the contest, thanks to him."

"I like a good upside-down, down-side-up, pineapple cake, but I just love a great right-side, left-side, cherry, chocolate-glazed, marble pie," slurped Jasper, filling the room with more of his stinky moose breath. "Mrs. Panosh brought me a winning piece. It was **delicious!**" he drooled. "**I just love** Mrs. Panosh."

"How dare that woman step into my kitchen and bring you some pie!" Mrs. Smythe screeched as she hacked up an onion into bits with a huge, steel-cutting knife. "How would she like it if I walked into her kitchen and fed that ridiculous rhinoceros mounted on her wall a piece of my upside-down, down-side-up, pineapple cake?"

"Rocco the rhinoceros can't eat your upside-down, down-side-up, pineapple cake," stated Jasper. "He's allergic to pineapples. He gets huge, red blotches all over his grey hide any time he goes near a pineapple. It's not a pretty sight at all, not pretty at all."

Mrs. Smythe's furious face became redder than her uniform as she went ranting and raving about the kitchen with a meat cleaver in her hand. The children ducked in fear for their lives as she swung it around screaming at Jasper.

"After you ruined my cake and had the nerve to eat Mrs. Panosh's pie, you're lucky I didn't hang you upside-down in the basement, you smelly thing." She threatened Jasper, chopping a head of lettuce perfectly into two chunks with the meat cleaver. "I was completely and utterly embarrassed having nothing to bring to the picnic. I'm not going to let Mrs. Panosh beat me again this year, I tell you! ***Not this year!***"

"My friend Grace is allergic to peanuts," Alexa said as she changed her hair into two pigtails. "If she goes anywhere near peanuts at all, she blows up like a balloon. No peanuts, peanut butter, peanut cookies, peanut butter and jelly sandwiches, peanut crackers, peanut cakes, peanut pie, peanut candy—nothing!"

"We get it, Lexy," moaned Jake. "We get it."

"When she comes over for a play date, we just have popcorn and apple juice," she added with a grin.

"*All this talk of food is making me dizzy*," Rex said, spinning around and then collapsing on the floor in disgust.

"Where are my manners?" Mrs. Smythe said, sharpening the end of her meat cleaver. "Let me fix you something to eat, you poor, little thing. I have a nice can of tuna in the cupboard that you will just love."

Not sure if he was getting a snack or if he was going to be chopped up into one, Rex, ever-so-hungry, but still cautious, scurried under Mrs. Smythe's apron over to the cupboard.

Jake continued to comb the room for clues with the magnifying glass. Though he was inspecting every inch of the floor, he was not paying much attention to a suit of armor that was beginning to walk right towards him. This suit had a red feather in its helmet, much like the blue one from the basement. Its shield had a red heart in the center, and the sword had a red ruby imbedded in the handle.

Alexa screamed, "Look out, Jake!" as the suit of armor

went crashing on top of him.

"Ouch!" he cried.

The red-feathered suit fell apart as it buried Jake. Red smoke went flying out of the rubble as the spirit of The Red Knight left the comfort of his suit of armor and began flying all around the vaulted ceilings of the kitchen.

Jake pushed the pile of armor off as he got up with the helmet of The Red Knight stuck on his head. He staggered around the room, bumping into every thing in his path, trying to pull the helmet off.

"Help, anyone!" he screamed in a muffled voice. "Are you guys still there?"

Alexa quickly ran to try to get the helmet off of Jake's head. "It's stuck, Jake!" she cried. "It's really stuck!" She pushed and pulled without any luck.

"Try moving the face shield," Jake directed. He looked like he was playing a crazy game of "pin the tail on the donkey" as he staggered blindly around the room with the heavy weight of the helmet pulling him down.

Alexa tried with all her strength to push the face shield up and over the helmet and finally managed to lift the face shield. Jake could see again, but the helmet was still stuck on his head.

Rex wobbled over to them with his belly popping out as it dragged on the floor. Overstuffed with tuna, he smirked, "*Nice hat!*" And then he burped.

"I think I liked you better when you couldn't talk!" exclaimed Jake as he yanked again on the helmet, still having no luck getting it off. "Delbert," he asked, "how many suits of armor did you say were in the museum?"

"Only five, Inspector, only five," Delbert answered.

"That makes two suits we've found so far," said Alexa, mesmerized by the red smoke of the spirit flying around the room. "The Blue Knight's suit from the basement and this helmet, which must belong to the suit of armor of The Red Knight."

"Lexy, there has to be a lever or button in the back of the helmet to get it open," Jake suggested.

Alexa ran around to the back of the helmet looking for something that would allow her to open it up. "There are no latches or buttons," she cried, "but there is a funny looking key hole back here."

"Just great! I'm going to be wearing this thing forever," he fussed. "I might as well go hang out in the basement with The Blue Knight."

Just then Jake remembered the keys they'd found in the basement near the other suit of armor. "Alexa, go get the keys we found in the basement. The ones engraved with the letter 'S', stashed in your backpack," he yelled. "Maybe we'll get lucky! The 'S' just might mean they're the keys to unlock the suits of armor."

Alexa ran to her backpack and pulled out the set of four keys. She then tried the first key in the helmet. "It fits!" she cried.

"Awesome!" mumbled Jake as the face shield slid once more over his face.

Alexa tried to turn the key, but it wouldn't budge.

"Sorry, Jake, that's not the right one," she said.

"There are only four keys, Inspector," said Delbert nervously. "But we have five suits of armor in the museum."

"I know, Delbert," said Jake. "That means one of the keys is missing."

"The missing key may be the one that opens this suit's helmet," moaned Alexa as she fiddled with the remaining keys.

"*Anyone got a can opener?*" Rex smirked.

"Rex, you are not using a can opener on my head!" Jake's voice echoed through the helmet.

Alexa proceeded with the second key but had no luck. She tried the third key, but it still did not open the helmet. "This is the fourth and last key we have," she exclaimed anxiously. At that moment, she put the fourth key into the helmet and gave it a turn. The helmet finally popped open and a look of relief came across everyone's faces.

"Yes!" Jake cried with happiness. When Jake turned his head to slide out, he saw Rex scurrying towards him. "Rex, give that can opener back to Mrs. Smythe," he yelled.

"*I was just going to open another can of tuna,*" muttered Rex *as* he slunk shamelessly back to Mrs. Smythe's gadget drawer. "*I wasn't going anywhere near your head—I promise!*"

Delbert, Jake, and Alexa proceeded to put together all the pieces from the red-feathered suit of armor.

Once they had finished placing the helmet back on top, the red hazy smoke flew down from above as the spirit of The Red Knight reentered his suit of armor. He adjusted his head a little to the right and walked off into the far corner of the kitchen.

"Delbert," Jake asked inquisitively as he jumped from

one black square on the floor to another. "How many people came to the museum last night?"

Delbert followed Jake's lead, jumping from one red square to another. "There were ten guests invited," he answered, "plus myself and Mrs. Smythe."

"When did you notice that time stopped and the bell was gone?" questioned Jake, leaping over a red square onto a new black one.

"It was sometime between seven o'clock and eight o'clock, because The Great Clock never rang after seven o'clock," Delbert said, hopping to the next red square. "When I noticed time had stopped, I immediately ran up the back stairwell to the clock tower to find The Bell of Time gone!"

Alexa became annoyed at being left out of the jumping game that Jake and Delbert had accidentally started to play. "If you two are going to play a game of human checkers, I want to play, too," she demanded.

"Oh!" said Delbert, all embarrassed, his face turning redder than the red checker square he was standing on. "I apologize for my rudeness, little lady. Would you care to play a game of checkers?"

"I think we'd better get back to solving this crime," interrupted Jake. But then he shouted "KING ME!" and flashed a grin towards his sister as he took one more leap onto a black square. "We really need to figure out where everyone was and what everyone was doing between seven and eight o'clock last night," Jake declared.

"At seven o'clock everyone was in the kitchen area having tea and Mrs. Smythe's famous lemon tarts," said

Delbert. "Lord Beasley was telling me how much he wished one day he could have my job and be The Keeper of Time. He thought it would be such fun controlling time."

"Lord Beasley especially enjoyed my lemon tarts," said Mrs. Smythe, brutally beating a small piece of baking dough with an oversized rolling pin. "He said they were the best batch yet! Shortly after that, The Duke of Snuffles became a little under the weather. I went to get his coat from the coat room, and he went home early from the party," she declared.

"He probably ate one of your sour lemon tarts and became sick to his stomach!" Jasper said, laughing himself silly.

"Hush up, you smelly moose!" she yelled, waving the rolling pin beneath his snout. "You're just mad because I wouldn't let you have one of my lemon tarts."

"What happened after The Duke of Snuffles left the museum?" interrupted Jake.

"I was *just* exhausted from the party," yawned Jasper. "I had to take a little nippy nap."

"I don't think the Inspector is interested in what you did last night, you hairy clod!" scolded Mrs. Smythe.

"Except for Lord Beasley, everyone else finished their dessert, and I escorted them all out the museum through the front door," said Delbert.

"What happened to Lord Beasley?" asked Alexa.

"I really don't have a clue," answered Delbert. "Lord Beasley was about to show Mrs. Smythe the beautifully monogrammed initials 'LB' on his black and white zebra-striped cashmere scarf that his mother gave him for his birthday. He went to grab his glasses, but he couldn't find them. Mrs. Smythe thought he had dropped them somewhere in the museum and suggested he go look for them. I assumed he found them and left."

"Did anyone actually see Lord Beasley's glasses last night?" asked Jake.

"No Inspector," said Mrs. Smythe, rummaging through her gadget drawer for something sharp to cut up her watermelon with. "I never even knew Lord Beasley wore glasses."

Delbert brushed some of Mrs. Smythe's mashed up potatoes off his captain's hat and added, "Neither did I!"

"Then we need to get to the scene of the crime," declared Jake. "If Lord Beasley was lying about having lost his glasses as an excuse to go running through the clock tower, then Lord Beasley just might be the criminal who stole time."

"Delbert," Jake asked, "you didn't see anything odd when you ran up to the clock tower last night?"

"I'm very embarrassed to say—no Inspector," answered Delbert politely. "I was so worried about The Bell of Time being stolen, I didn't pay much attention to anything else. I'm terribly sorry."

"That's O.K. Delbert; that's why you have me here!" exclaimed Jake, twirling the magnifying glass in his hand. "After all, mysterious crimes are my specialty! Did you see Lord Beasley actually leave, Mrs. Smythe?"

"Oh, no, Inspector," confessed Mrs. Smythe, still searching her kitchen for just the right culinary tool to slice her watermelon. "I was in the back butler's pantry refilling my baking drawers with flour and baking soda to get ready to bake my cake for the contest. Though I was sick and tired of hearing Lord Beasley brag on and on about that silly scarf. You'd think it was made of gold the way he carried on about it. Why I have one just like it. It's nothing special."

Jake and Alexa put the keys back into the backpack. Mrs. Smythe, unable to find the perfect sharp instrument to cut up the watermelon, began to ferociously gather up pots and pans for baking her famous, award-winning, upside-down, down-side-up, pineapple cake.

"While you're trying to solve this mystery in the clock tower, I will try baking my cake," she said. "Though I don't know how well it will come out. Without time, I really won't know how long to bake it."

"Jasper," she said with a devilish smile, "do you remember that counting game we played last time I baked my cake?"

Jasper was pretending to be snoring.

"**JASPER!**" she yelled. "I know you're awake, and you're going to help me win, with or without time working! You count to a thousand Mississippi's again for me, just like last time. You'll have to be my clock. By the time you finish counting, the cake should be done baking."

"Only if I get to eat the leftover lemon tarts," he begged with his big tongue dangling over the mantel, just barely avoiding getting singed from the fireplace's bright, orange flames.

"Well, don't eat too many of them," she joked with an evil grin. "I wouldn't want you to get sick to your stomach!"

The Red Knight clanked loudly as it passed Mrs. Smythe. Jake and Alexa looked up at the long, stone, spiral staircase leading from the kitchen to the clock tower.

"This will do," stated Mrs. Smythe as she grabbed The Red Knight's sword and sliced and diced her watermelon into a hundred pieces.

"Watermelon, anyone!" she bellowed with a deliciously wicked smile.

"No, thank you," echoed the children nervously as Delbert quickly guided them from the kitchen into the stairway up to the clock tower.

chapter
five
Lights Out

It was cold and windy in the stairway; the storm was approaching the museum. Jake and Alexa were exhausted following Delbert up the endless steps on their journey to the clock tower high above. The children stopped to catch their breath on a landing half way between the kitchen and the clock tower. As they passed an open doorway filled with cobwebs and creepy crawling spiders, they noticed a flickering light beyond.

"Where are we, Delbert?" asked Alexa, brushing the cobwebs from her hair.

"This is The Library of Time, filled with books all about clocks and time," he whispered.

"*Why are you whispering?*" whispered Rex.

"The librarian gets very cranky when you interrupt his work," Delbert said softly. "He was as mad as mad could be when all the guests were walking through there last night messing with his books."

With his magnifying glass, Jake examined every corner of the door for clues and then started to make his way into the room. "Aren't you coming, Delbert?" he asked.

Delbert became very nervous and started to shake so

much three clocks on his red suspenders fell to the ground. "Oh, no, Inspector, I never go into the library," he said. "The librarian and I really don't get along very well. You go ahead. I'll wait out here." He picked up his clocks and stood there ashamed of his lack of bravery.

"*Maybe I should stay out here, too!*" purred Rex, curling around Delbert's legs.

"Yeah, me too!" said Alexa.

"No way," said Jake as he dragged her while kicking Rex on the butt to move him along. "If I'm going, you're going!"

They tip-toed ever-so-cautiously, not sure of what they would find beyond the doorway. Except for a flickering light in the deepest corner of the room, it was as dark as night.

"If we can't see anything in here, we won't be able to look for clues," Jake suggested, squinting his eyes. "We need to find a light switch."

"It's five steps to your right, Inspector!" a very deep voice said slowly from inside the dark.

Jumping into Jake's arms, Rex's fur puffed up again and his eyes opened as wide as they could. He stared toward the voice, shaking like a caught mouse. Jake started to worry, knowing Rex could see in the dark.

"What do you see?" Jake whispered to Rex.

"*I'm not sure,*" he whispered back, "*but I know it's not good!*"

"It's five steps to your right, Inspector," the voice slowly repeated.

Jake proceeded to move slowly five steps to the right, with Alexa holding onto his shirt tail close behind. Jake searched the wall until he found the light switch and pushed it up. Nothing happened. The children continued to stand in the darkness of the library.

"Hey, you said the light switch was five steps to the right!" complained Jake, turning the switch up and down.

"And you said **you** were looking for a light **switch**, Inspector!" said the voice from beyond. "Not lights."

Alexa was getting a little mad at this point and didn't care how scary the voice sounded. She screamed, "**Alright**, let's try this again! How do we *turn* on the lights so *we* can see?"

At that moment huge flashes of blinding light exploded from the tall ceiling as if a series of fireworks were going off above their heads. The lights were so bright it took a while for Jake and Alexa to adjust their eyes.

"In order to get the right answers, you have to ask the right questions," explained the voice.

The children were amazed and confused. Except for very thick glasses dangling from his nose, the tiniest of silver letters pinned on his green suspenders, and a black, shiny top hat crookedly sitting on top of his head, the librarian looked exactly like Delbert.

Jake thought to himself, it can't be. Delbert, after all, was waiting outside the library. Or was he?

The library looked like a tornado had hit it. It was filled with thousands and thousands of old, dusty books—some of them stacked miles high and others just thrown about. Jake and Alexa started flipping through the books and noticed that all the books were about just one thing—**time**. The strange, little man looked up, squinting through his thick glasses as he tried to focus on the children standing in the glare of the bright lights. "I am Rupert, the librarian," he said slowly in his very deep voice. "This is The Library of Time. How may I be of service to you, Inspector?"

"Funny," giggled Alexa as she braided a strand of hair, "except for the glasses, you look a lot like Delbert."

Rupert crinkled his forehead, raising his eyebrows beyond the thin gold metal frames of his very thick glasses, and declared, "**Well I should!** Delbert's my brother, my twin brother. He's older by four and a half minutes. Time was not on my side that day," he explained, slamming the gigantic dictionary of time he was reading. "My Grandfather was The Keeper of Time, and his job was supposed to go to his first born grandson."

Jake began examining the dictionary with the magnifying glass as Rex whispered in his ear. "*This guy's got one too many loose cuckoo clocks in his brain. We need to get out of here!*"

"I'm with Rex on this one, Jake," Alexa whispered back.

Jake looked at them both with an annoyed look on his face. "We came here to solve a crime, and a crime we will— solve!" he said firmly. "The Moustachios aren't quitters."

Rupert was paying absolutely no attention to them as he fumbled around the endless stacks of books, slamming open ones shut with a forceful thud as he continued to tell his never-ending story. "If Delbert hadn't been born first, I would be The Keeper of Time and he would be stuck in this library every day categorizing and alphabetizing these darn books about time and minutes and chimes and clocks and hours and days," he whined ever-so-loudly.

"It never ends. Day after day after day, new boxes of books arrive, always filled with the same thing, endless books about time for me to categorize and alphabetize. My job never ends. **But** — it will soon," he said with an evil grin as he slammed shut another book. "With time missing, I won't get any more new books, and I will finally complete my task. Delbert promised me when I finish categorizing and alphabetizing all the books then I will get to be the next Keeper of Time."

"And what happens to Delbert?" asked Alexa nervously.

"He becomes the librarian," Rupert announced, laughing so hard he knocked over three piles of books. "It's only fair!"

As Jake continued looking for clues through his magnifying glass around the library, he thought to himself that Rupert could have taken The Bell of Time. He had the chance. No one would ever have seen him steal time with the library being so close to the clock tower. He had motive. With time stopped, he would be able to finish his work and become the new Keeper of Time. But did he do it? And was he really Rupert, the librarian, or was he Delbert in disguise?

Jake decided to examine Rupert's face closer, hoping to answer some of his own questions. He noticed Rupert was wearing an odd scarf. It was a black and white zebra print, much like the one Mrs. Smythe observed Lord Beasley wearing last night. "Rupert," he said, "that is a very unusual scarf you are wearing."

"Isn't it, though?" he replied, loosening it up from around his neck. "I just love the material, cashmere, you know. It keeps me very warm when I do my work."

Rupert took the scarf off and gave it to Jake to feel how soft it was. With the help of the magnifying glass, Jake immediately noticed the embroidered initials "L.B." This confirmed his suspicions that the scarf was, in fact, Lord Beasley's.

Jake thought to himself, how did Rupert get Lord Beasley's scarf?

"Rupert," he asked, "how long have you had this scarf?"

"Since last night," Rupert replied as he grabbed back the scarf, wrapping it ever-so-tightly around his stumpy neck. "I found it outside my door when I put out my dinner tray for Mrs. Smythe to pick up. She always brings me dinner at five o'clock, and I always leave my dinner tray outside the library door at seven-fifteen sharp so she can pick it up and return it to the kitchen."

"Did you hear or see anything strange last night?" asked Jake as he tried to figure out how to get that scarf back from Rupert.

"I heard a lot of ruckus up and down the stairs, but I saw nothing," answered Rupert, squinting as he cleaned his glasses off with the edge of the scarf. "I never, ever leave the library, you know, way too much work to do. Plus, I'm as blind as blind can be. My brother got the better set of eyes. I can barely see anything, even with these darn glasses of mine," he declared as he put them back on, still not able to see the children very well.

Jake understood now. Because of his poor eyesight, Rupert never saw Lord Beasley's tiny initials on the scarf when he took it to keep warm. It was becoming clearer to Jake that Lord Beasley must have dropped his scarf as he was running from the scene of the crime. As he examined the scarf for clues, he noticed a strange smell in the room. "What's that smell?" he said.

"*Sorry, I ate a few lemon tarts with my tuna, not a good mix—very gassy,*" said Rex as his furry cheeks turned red from embarrassment.

"Not you, you crazy fur ball," scolded Jake. "I smelled you a while ago."

"*Hey, try sleeping next to you after a pickle and mustard sandwich. It doesn't smell pretty either!*" Rex yelled back.

Jake proceeded to sniff the scarf behind Rupert's neck without him noticing.

Vanilla, he thought to himself. This scarf smells like vanilla!

Jake signaled Alexa and Rex to come smell the scarf on the back of Rupert's neck. Alexa picked up Rex, and they took a deep breath. "***Vanilla!***" they confirmed.

"Rupert, have you eaten anything with vanilla since you found the scarf?" Alexa asked, her head buried in her backpack as she searched for a new hair tie.

"No, I haven't, young lady," Rupert answered.

Jake was puzzled over how or why Lord Beasley's scarf came to smell like vanilla. He was surer than ever that he needed the scarf as evidence to solve this mystery. "Rupert, may I have this scarf?" he asked politely. "It may be just what I need to solve this crime."

"Certainly not!" shouted Rupert as he clung on to the scarf, outraged. "I need it to keep me warm, and I don't want you to solve the crime before I've finished my work. How else will I become the new Keeper of Time?"

Jake and Alexa looked around the room and knew there was not a chance Rupert would ever be able to finish his work before they solved the case. All the books were alphabetized and categorized wrong. The A's were next to the Z's, and the F's were next to the Y's.

"Well, Rupert, you got us there. It looks like you will be definitely finished with your job before I am with mine!" kidded Jake. "So how about we make a deal? I will trade you something that will keep you warmer, and you give me the scarf."

Rupert raised his eyebrows in anticipation of what Jake was going to give him. Jake excused himself as he and Alexa went to the back of the library for a private meeting.

"I need another scarf from your Inspector Girl backpack to make a trade," he explained.

"I don't have a scarf in here!" she stammered, rummaging through her backpack. "It's not like I carry one with me. Why does every one think I always have what they need in here?"

"Except for my tuna, you usually do have everything in here," said Rex, jumping into the backpack to help.

"The cat's right. You're just like Grandma Moustachio. You always have anything and everything in your backpack," Jake said.

Alexa pulled Rex out of her backpack and stuck her

hand in, searching for something good to trade with Rupert. "No luck on the scarf, but I do have a pink snow hat!" she exclaimed.

Jake smirked as he grabbed it and said, "That'll do!"

Suddenly, a crack of thunder frightened the children as the storm approached outside the tower walls. They jumped in fear from the roaring sound, knocking over a pile of books that toppled onto them. While pulling the books off themselves, they were startled by another suit of armor that clanked past them. This one was a little more eerie and taller than the blue one in the basement or the red one in the kitchen. It had a large, green, fluffy feather sticking out of the steel-plated helmet. The small, green diamonds painted across the shield glistened against the bright lights of the library. The extremely sharp, green-striped blade of the sword made the children tremble in fear.

Jake gave Alexa a brotherly smile, "We can't be afraid, Lexy. We have a case to solve. We have to check everywhere we can for clues to solving this crime. That includes inside that green-feathered suit of armor. Quick, grab the keys," he shouted.

Alexa trembled as she reached into her backpack, pulling out the set of four keys with the letter "S" on them. "I'm on it, Inspector!"

As she tossed the keys to Jake, she caught the strap on her backpack on the green, diamond shield of the suit of armor. Misty, green smoke started to puff out of the steel faceplate of the helmet. The spirit of The Green Knight came alive, looking like a fire-breathing dragon about to attack its prey. The Green Knight, paying no attention to the hooked backpack, continued to move with it hanging from his shield. Alexa bravely tried to grab it but got tangled up in the strap.

She and the backpack were both trapped, hanging from the suit of armor as it continued to clank across the room, breathing green smoke out of the nose of its cold, steel-plated helmet.

"Ahhhhhhhhhh!" screamed Alexa. "Jake, help me. I'm caught!"

"I'm coming, Lex!" yelled Jake as he puffed up his chest and raised his clenched hands in a fist, ready to take on the spirit of The Green Knight.

Just at that moment, Rex got a burst of cat courage when he saw his Alexa in grave danger. He quickly jumped up on top of a pile of books like a ferocious lion and leaped into the air, onto the suit of armor. He grabbed on with his little paws for dear life as he swung back and forth from the helmet's fluffy, green feather.

"Help!" yelled Rex. *"Help!"*

"Oh, brother!" sighed Jake, holding his hand above his head, shaking it in disbelief. "Now I have to save both of you!"

Jake ran as fast as he could to catch up with them. When he got closer, he slid face first between the legs of the green-feathered suit, hitting the corner of the wall. Rex and Alexa were dangling and swaying as the spirit of The Green Knight clanked across the floor getting closer and closer to Jake. Dazed, Jake stood up. He was trapped as he saw the suit of armor raising his sharp sword, pointing it towards him.

"Lexy— stop him!" cried Jake as he covered his eyes.

"He's going to stab me to death!"

Another roar of thunder shook the fragile stone walls of the tower. Alexa and Rex tried every thing they could to get the sword away, but it wouldn't budge. They, too, closed their eyes, too scared to watch what was about to happen.

They all let out huge screams as the sharp, green-edged sword swung fiercely towards Jake's head. Then, to their great surprise, there was only silence as the suit of armor came to rest.

Shaking, too afraid to remove his hands from covering his eyes, Jake muttered, "Am I still alive?"

Jumping down from the bent, green feather, Rex said, *"And you thought only cats had nine lives!"*

Unharmed, Jake ran to untangle Alexa from the strap. As she climbed down, she noticed The Green Knight's sword had stabbed a book that was on top of a pile of books in the corner where Jake had been trapped.

Jake rushed to pull the sword out from the book. "I don't think The Green Knight was coming for me, after all," he said. "If he had wanted to finish me off, he could have. Instead, he chose to stab this book."

"But, why this book?" questioned Alexa as she flipped through the stabbed pages.

Jake read aloud the title of the book, *A False Knight in Time*. The spirit of The Green Knight must be trying to tell us something about The Bell of Time. This has to be a clue to solving the case and restoring time."

The Green Knight stumbled over to Jake and stuck out his hand. Jake looked puzzled for a second and then realized he wanted his sword back. Trembling as he handed back the sword, he said, "I think this belongs to you."

The Green Knight took back his sword and left the confines of the tired, old, rusty, green-feathered suit of armor. The green, hazy smoke of his spirit swirled around and around the children's heads and then finally went flying off into the bookshelves of The Library of Time.

"Now is our chance to search the suit," cried Jake, fumbling with the keys. He tried all the keys except for the one that he knew unlocked the red-feathered suit of armor from the kitchen. On the second key, the helmet opened right up. Jake grabbed his magnifying glass and looked inside to find nothing but cobwebs and dust.

"That makes three suits we've found so far. Two of which we've opened—this one belonging to The Green Knight and The Red Knight's suit from the kitchen. The only one we haven't tried to open yet is The Blue Knight's suit in the basement," he said.

"And we have two more suits we haven't found yet. The Purple Knight's suit and The Yellow Knight's suit," said Alexa, placing the keys and the book safely in her Inspector Girl backpack.

"Don't forget one missing key!" Rex reminded them.

"I don't know how, but something is telling the detective in me that those keys, that book, Lord Beasley's scarf, and the suits of armor are somehow connected to the disappearance of time," said Jake. "That missing key, if we ever do find it, *just* might help us solve this crime."

"Well, if anyone can solve this crime, it is The Great Inspector Moustachio!" said Alexa as she zipped up her backpack, throwing it over her shoulder.

"Your Grandpa would be proud of both of you," said Rex smiling.

"We need to get that scarf and get up to the clock tower, fast!" Jake exclaimed.

Jake and Alexa ran back through the maze of books to Rupert, with Rex scurrying close behind them. They offered to trade him the pink hat for Lord Beasley's zebra-striped scarf. He gladly accepted, though with his bad eyesight he never realized it was pink. As the children left the library, the lights blew out as mysteriously as they had exploded on. There was only that tiny flickering light above Rupert's head as he got back to his work.

"I can see better in the dark," he said. "And remember, Inspector, in order to get the right answers, you have to ask the right questions!"

"I won't forget, Rupert," said Jake. "Thanks!"

The children made their way through the darkness of the library back to the staircase with the keys, the book and the scarf safely tucked away in Alexa's backpack. Delbert was anxiously awaiting their return from the library.

"Guess what, Delbert?" exclaimed Alexa. "We found Lord Beasley's scarf and The Green Knight's suit of armor."

"And we found your brother," said Jake suspiciously as he examined every inch of Delbert with the magnifying glass, trying to determine if they were really twins at all.

"Oh, dear!" sighed Delbert. "How is Rupert doing today?"

"He thinks he's about to become the new Keeper of Time," Jake said. "But don't worry; I'll have this caper wrapped up before he's finished with those books."

"I certainly hope so, Inspector. I can't imagine Time keeping on time with Rupert watching over it," pondered Delbert. "I just love my brother, but as you can see his eyesight is not so good."

"Well, then," said Jake, "I guess we should get to the scene of the crime."

chapter six

A Honk And A Sneeze

Delbert led the children further up the winding stairs to the clock tower above. The storm was definitely upon them. It felt like a bolt of lighting and a rumble of thunder were shaking through them to their tippy toes. They arrived at a huge black door with a sparkling door knob that reminded Alexa of her mother's pretty earrings. Slowly, Delbert turned the wobbly knob. The only light to see with was coming from the lightning outside the large, rainbow, stained-glass window with a broken latch. With every gust of wind, the window kept banging and banging against the high stone walls of the clock tower. Passing Delbert, Jake, Alexa, and Rex tip-toed ever-so-cautiously into the tower.

All of a sudden, a crack of lighting hit the top of the clock tower, with a roar of thunder right behind it. A gigantic gust of wind blew through the open window, knocking Delbert off his feet, causing him to fall backwards into the doorway. The force of the wind slammed the giant door shut so hard that the door knobs fell off, trapping Jake, Alexa, and Rex inside.

"That's just great!" whined Rex. *"We're trapped in the*

dark up here, and I'm going to need a litter box real soon."

"No one told you to go eating tuna and lemon tarts at the same time," scolded Alexa.

"Hush up, you guys," said Jake. "I can't hear Delbert."

"Inspector, are you O.K.?" he asked from the other side of the door.

"Yes, Delbert, we can hear you," yelled Jake. "We can't open the door from this side. Can you open it up from your side?"

Delbert felt all around him, but could not find the door knob.

"I can't find the knob from this side," he said. "How about you?"

"It's too dark!" yelled back Jake as he, too, crawled around on his side of the door looking for the door knob. "Where are the lights?"

"The storm must have blown out the electricity. There are no lights on in the stairs either," yelled Delbert. "I will go get some help."

Delbert carefully felt his way down the stairs, trying not to stumble. Jake, Alexa, and Rex stood still in the darkness of the clock tower, too scared to move.

"Rex," Jake moaned, "your breath stinks. Stop breathing on me." At that moment a gigantic sneeze filled the room. "Rex, that's so gross. Find a tissue!" he scolded.

"I'm down here!" snarled Rex, swatting Jake on the knee with his paw.

"Ah—oh," cried Jake as another huge **A—AH CHOOOOOOOO** filled the air.

The children and Rex let out a huge scream as they ran

for their lives, getting as far away from the sneezing as they could.

Alexa quickly grabbed the flashlight in her backpack, but it wouldn't turn on. "I'm not sure—it's so dark in here— but I think the flashlight's broken," she said.

"*Great! Now what do we do?*" asked Rex as he sat on top of Jake's head.

"Wait, I have an idea!" shrieked Alexa, rummaging through her backpack, pulling out a weird-looking box. "Glow sticks! Glow sticks!" she exclaimed. "I have glow sticks!"

"*Now let me get this straight. You didn't bring my tuna or my litter box, but you have glow sticks in there,*" Rex moaned, jumping off Jake's head.

"Well, it's a good thing we've got them," said Jake. "Now hurry, let's start cracking them and lay them around the tower so we can see what's out there!"

Jake and Alexa cracked all the glow sticks as fast as they could. Rex grabbed them with his paws and threw them across the clock tower's floor. The tower and the magnificent Great Clock of Grimthorpe quickly glowed with beautiful colors of neon pinks, yellows, oranges, and greens.

"Pretty colors," said a mysterious sweet voice.

Jake, Alexa, and Rex looked up through the rainbow haze and saw a pretty lady sitting upon a large, white goose, knitting what appeared to be a mitten. They both were wearing pink airplane pilot goggles and matching white, leather, bomber jackets. The trio stood there too scared to move as the goose started to flap her wings.

"What pretty colors!" said the lady as she jumped off

the goose, still knitting away. The goose, which was holding an enormous rainbow-colored ball of yarn, let out a large honk and another sneeze, causing the ball to roll towards the children's feet. The lady had the most beautiful, long, golden-blond hair and sparkling, blue eyes, reminding Jake and Alexa of their mother.

"*That was disgusting,*" snapped Rex as he started swatting the big ball of yarn. "*Get that enormous duck a tissue. Ewe— I just hate animal germs.*"

"You're an animal," smirked Jake, "and that's not a duck; it's a goose."

"*I like to think of myself as a four-legged person who happens to have a lot of fur!*" Rex announced, rolling on top of the rainbow ball of yarn.

"How many people do you know cough up fur balls and go to the bathroom in sand?" snapped Jake.

"*O.K, you win on the fur balls, but have you seen the playground at school, lately? There has definitely been some sand-box peeing in there,*" Rex replied, snapping the ball with his tail.

"Don't worry, everyone. Gertrude doesn't have a cold, just some allergies to certain powders," said the pretty lady, still feverishly knitting away. The goose then let out another enormous honk and sneezed.

"You know, my friend Grace has allergies, too—" said Alexa as she pulled a loose strand of yarn from the ball, braiding it through her hair. "If she goes anywhere near peanuts at all, she blows up like a balloon. No peanuts, peanut butter, peanut cookies, peanut butter and jelly sandwiches, peanut crackers, peanut cakes, peanut pie, peanut candy—nothing!"

"We know, already. We know!" shouted Jake and Rex in exasperation.

"Oh, where are my manners?" the lady asked as her mitten got larger and larger with every turn of her knitting needles. "This is Gertrude, and I am Mrs. Panosh."

Stunned, they let out a scream of excitement, "Mrs. Panosh!!!!"

"You mean, *The* Mrs. Panosh who won last year's town picnic's baking contest with her right-side, left-side, cherry, chocolate-glazed, marble pie!" exclaimed Alexa.

Mrs. Panosh walked over to Alexa and knelt down and said, "Why, yes, dear. And who are you?"

"I'm Alexa Moustachio, and this is my brother, Inspector Jake Moustachio, and our cat, Rex. We are here to find The Bell of Time."

"What adorable sleuths you all are," said Mrs. Panosh, handing the huge ball of yarn to Alexa. "I just love a good mystery."

Alexa loved to knit. She was so excited watching Mrs. Panosh finish her rainbow mitten. Alexa carefully unwound the ball of yarn on one end as Mrs. Panosh knitted the ball into the most beautiful mitten she had ever seen.

"You're such good detectives; you already know who I am. And, more importantly, you know how wonderful I bake. Tell me, tell me, who told you all about me?" Mrs. Panosh asked with much pride.

"Jasper," said Jake, examining every inch as he climbed up into The Great Clock of Grimthorpe to look for clues with his magnifying glass.

"Oh, Jasper, my dear old friend, Jasper," she sighed.

"How is he doing with that horribly wicked woman, Mrs. Smythe?"

"I guess you and Mrs. Smythe aren't the best of buddies?" Jake's voice echoed from inside the face of the clock.

"Certainly not!" yelled Mrs. Panosh. "That woman stole my cooking job here at the museum and moved right into my kitchen."

"How did she do that?" questioned Alexa, trying not to get the yarn all tangled up.

"Well, five years ago she moved into town and entered her upside-down, down-side-up, pineapple cake into the town baking contest," she explained. "Why, I am the best baker in the world. I had always won the baking contest before she arrived. My pastries, pies, and cakes have been eaten by royalty for years. She was jealous and wanted to win, no matter what, even if she had to cheat! Mrs. Smythe placed her cake right next to my famous pie and, though I've never been able to prove it, I know she was the one who sprinkled hot black pepper all over the top. The black pepper looked just like my chocolate sprinkles. When the judges took one bite, they became sick to their stomachs. She poisoned them. I was the laughing stock of the town. My pristine baking reputation was ruined. I was fired from my job here at the museum."

"*Oh no—,*" moaned Rex as he staggered across the tower, clutching his throat. "*I ate one of the poisonous lemon tarts that The Duke of Snuffles ate. I'm—dying. I'm as doomed as doomed as can be. It's getting dark in here. I see strange lights and strange animals. The end is near!*"

"You're the only strange animal here," scolded Alexa. "And you weren't poisoned, and you're not dying!"

"And if you don't knock it off, I'm going to drop you off at the dog pound when we get home," threatened Jake, crawling out of the clock.

"*Never mind!*" sighed Rex, scratching his back with a pink glow stick.

"Please continue, Mrs. Panosh," Jake said.

"After that, the only job I could get was cooking for the animals at the town zoo!" she said sadly. "I went from baking for royalty to mixing mush for animals. Could you imagine the humiliation?"

"Honk!" went Gertrude, flapping her wings annoyingly throughout the clock tower.

"Sorry, Gerty," Mrs. Panosh said apologetically. "It's not that I don't love you and all the other animals; it's just not the same as being here in the museum."

"But you won the baking contest last year," said Jake.

"That's right, Inspector, I did!" Mrs. Panosh exclaimed. "I finally got my revenge after all these years. I must admit I was a bit naughty, but Mrs. Smythe deserved it. Just as I did tonight, Gertrude and I flew into the bell tower through that window with the broken latch. No one knows this place better than I. I lived here for many years. I know every room, stair, and secret passageway that there is."

"*That could come in handy!*" exclaimed Rex, nipping at the yarn.

"I knew Jasper couldn't resist eating cake and getting Mrs. Smythe mad. The day she baked her cake for the contest I snuck into the kitchen, down the secret back tunnel passage, right behind that picture of Lord Grimthorpe over there," she said, pointing to the picture.

"I put her cake on the mantel, right under Jasper's nose. He gobbled it up in no time. With no cake for the contest, I won. That's exactly what I intend to do tonight as soon as she finishes that awful upside-down, down-side-up, pineapple cake."

"*You know vanilla baking powder is her secret ingredient,*" said Rex, now completely tangled up in the yarn.

"Mrs. Panosh," Jake asked as he meticulously examined every speck of her for clues, "may I ask where you were last night?"

"I had nothing to do with The Bell of Time missing," she snapped. "I was home with the animals. Why, I do believe I was measuring Gertrude's feet for the mittens I'm knitting. She gets very cold feet this time of year. Don't you, Gerty?"

Gertrude let out a loud honk and a horrific sneeze.

"*Was that a honk for **yes** or a sneeze for **no** on the mittens?*" asked Rex.

"Why don't you question Mrs. Smythe about the missing bell?" said Mrs. Panosh. "I'll bet my entire collection of recipe books she had something to do with this mystery.

"If you ask the right questions, you'll always get the right answers."

That's funny, Jake thought to himself. Rupert said the same thing.

"Mrs. Panosh, what kind of powder is Gertrude allergic to, exactly?" Jake asked.

"Oh, corn starch, baby powder, vanilla, and oatmeal powder," she answered.

Jake thought how odd it was for Gertrude to be sneezing in the clock tower. He remembered the vanilla smell on Lord Beasley's scarf. Maybe he did do it, but why? Did Rupert pretend to be Lord Beasley by wearing his scarf and taking The Bell of Time so he could finish his work and become the next Keeper of Time? Did Mrs. Smythe grab the bell to prevent anyone from baking their cakes for the contest so she could win? Or was Mrs. Panosh lying to cover her tracks and to frame Mrs. Smythe so she could get her job back at the museum?

He knew his detective skills were bringing him closer to solving this crime, but where exactly did the vanilla powder, the book from the library, the keys, and the suits of armor all fit into the crime? He wondered.

All of a sudden, it dawned on him as he grabbed a glow stick and ran excitedly with his magnifying glass throughout the clock tower, examining every nook and cranny for clues. "The person who took the bell must have been covered in vanilla powder. That's why Gertrude is sneezing. There must be vanilla powder somewhere around here!" Jake exclaimed. "If we find the trail, it might just lead us to The Bell of Time."

Jake went over to examine the portrait of Lord Grimthorpe. He was a swashbuckling old guy, with a gigantic, brown safari hat resting just off to one side of his head. He had a golden-brown mustache that was waxed into two perfect curls at the sides of his nose.

Jake heard a lot of clanking coming from behind the picture and sounds of something moving around in the back tunnel. "How do we get into the secret passageway?" he inquired of Mrs. Panosh.

"Just press on Lord Grimthorpe's nose, my dear!" she informed him as she knotted the last piece of yarn needed for Gertrude's mittens. Alexa rolled up the remainder of the yarn and handed the still gigantic ball back to Mrs. Panosh, who then tucked it away in Gertrude's deep feathers.

Jake pressed on Lord Grimthorpe's nose. The gray, mossy, stone wall opened up, leading to the secret tunnel beyond the clock tower. Just then, another bolt of lighting struck, and a rumble of thunder sounded in the dark skies above the clock tower. The clanking noise got louder and louder as the last two suits of armor, one with a yellow feather and one with a purple feather, came trudging through.

These two suits were much bigger and meaner looking than the last three they had encountered. Jake remembered almost being stabbed by the green-feathered suit in the library and became very frightened as the two suits entered. The purple one had purple stripes running down its shield with a purple dagger instead of a sword. The yellow one had four yellow squares on its shield. It stood there holding a threatening crossbow.

"*They look a little angry!*" exclaimed Rex as he hid behind Gertrude.

"I think you're right," said Alexa as she hid behind Rex hiding behind Gertrude.

The spirits of The Yellow and Purple Knights stared down at Jake as they surrounded him. He was too scared to move as the misty, yellow and purple smoke of both the spirits' eyes glowed behind their cold, steel helmets. Knowing he had a crime to solve, Jake took a brave, deep breath and whispered to Alexa to get the keys.

"I don't think this is a good idea," said Rex, trembling as he hid under Gertrude's feathers.

Alexa slowly grabbed the keys from her backpack. Jake cautiously slipped the untried keys into each of the helmets, opening both successfully. Neither suit made a movement as the spirits flew out of their suits. They danced around the rafters of the clock tower's ceiling, causing an explosion of color as their purple and yellow smoke blended with the light radiating from the glow sticks. It was as if the spirits were inviting Jake to check out the suits of armor for clues to unravel the mystery. Jake boosted Alexa up and she looked into one of the suits.

"Empty!" echoed throughout the tower as Alexa pulled her head out of the purple-feathered one.

Mrs. Panosh was so excited by the events that she, too, checked out the yellow-feathered one. It was also empty.

"We need to get out of here, fast, before these spirits start to get angry. We need to get to the first suit of armor in the basement and find that darn missing key," shouted Jake. "Mrs. Panosh, can you get us to the basement through this passageway?"

"I would be delighted to my dear. With this storm upon us, Gerty and I won't be flying out any time soon. This is so exciting!" exclaimed Mrs. Panosh. "It's like being in my favorite board game, House Detective. I just love to scream out the criminal at the end of the game. General Ketchup, in the bedroom, with the rope!"

Rex stuck his head out from under his hiding place in Gertrude's feathers, looking at Mrs. Panosh as if she were crazy.

"That's my favorite game, too!" exclaimed Alexa, snatching Rex out from Gertrude. "I love it when it's Miss Pumpernickel, in the garden, with the candlestick."

chapter seven

Goose Race

While the spirits of the Purple and Yellow Knights danced around the clock tower ceiling, everyone grabbed a glow stick and proceeded through the opening of the secret passageway to the tunnel beyond. The tunnel was a cold, damp, musty maze with dead ends leading to nowhere. Mrs. Panosh explained that during The Great War of Antwerp, the army frequently hid their spare armor and weapons from the enemy in secret compartments throughout the maze of the tunnel.

"What's that rattling noise?" asked Alexa as she felt her way through the eerie trail.

"It must be the echo of the spirits of the Purple and Yellow Knights reentering their suits of armor," deduced Jake.

Gertrude let out a large honk and bunches of sneezes.

"*Is that duck with us, too?*" moaned Rex. "*This is turning into a parade.*"

"Rex, stop your whining," demanded Jake. "Gertrude's sneezes are going to lead us to the trail of vanilla powder left by the culprit who took the bell."

As the group continued to walk down through the tunnel, they heard a loud crunch.

"Ah, no!" yelled Jake.

"What was that?" Alexa inquired.

"I stepped on something," he said. "I hope that wasn't the bell."

"*We are in deep cat litter if it was!*" Rex sighed.

Jake searched the floor in the dark, trying to use the magnifying glass in what light he could get from the glow stick, to find what he had crushed with his foot. "Got it!" he shouted. "It's not the bell but a pair of glasses."

"Why would there be a pair of glasses in the secret tunnel?" asked Mrs. Panosh.

"These must be Lord Beasley's glasses," said Jake.

"*So he did do it!*" deduced Rex.

"He must have dropped the scarf Rupert found on his way up the stairway to the tower," said Alexa.

"*And then stole The Bell of Time,*" said Rex.

"And then made his escape through this tunnel, dropping his glasses as he ran from the scene of the crime," said Alexa. "You did it Jake! You did it! You solved the crime!"

"My detective skills are telling me something is wrong here. We still don't know where the bell is. But the keys and these suits of armor are somehow involved in the mystery; I just know it!" Jake said.

"And what about the book from the library and the vanilla powder everywhere? It doesn't make sense yet." Jake handed the broken glasses to Alexa. She put them in her backpack with the rest of the clues, the set of four "S" marked keys, the book from the library, *A False Knight in Time*, and Lord Beasley's scarf.

Gertrude's continuous sneezing was echoing against the stone wall of the tunnels.

"There must be a trail of vanilla powder on the floor that we can't see in the dark," said Jake.

"*Tha—a—a—t rattling is getting louder!*" stuttered Rex.

"Which way, Mrs. Panosh?" asked Jake.

"To the right, dear. To the right," she directed.

As they turned right into the next passageway, the rattling was getting louder and louder from all sides.

"I don't like this at all, you guys," shouted Jake. "There is way too much rattling and clanking for it to be coming from just two suits of armor."

The glow sticks were starting to fade, and the tunnel was getting darker and darker by the second. Gertrude's sneezes were getting more frequent as they penetrated deeper and deeper into the maze.

"*Now, we really are in deep cat litter!*" exclaimed Rex, jumping back into the deep feathers of Gertrude to hide.

The group stopped at a crossroads in the middle of the tunnel's maze. The Knights were coming from behind them, in front of them, to the right of them, and to the left of them.

"*We're trapped,*" screamed Rex. "*We're doomed! We're doomed!*"

The Knights were right on top of them. Alexa quickly reached for the flashlight to see if it would work. She gave the lever one good push, and it came on, giving them a tiny beam of light in the dark terror of the tunnel. They were cornered. The Yellow Knight was behind them. The Green Knight was to the left. The Red Knight was to their right and The Purple Knight blocked their path ahead.

Alexa let out a horrified scream as a large, steel hand came from behind The Purple Knight and plucked her right out from the center of the group. The flashlight went flying in the air, crashing on the ground as the suit of armor carried her off into the dark distance of the tunnel.

"Jake, help me!" she screamed into the darkness.

"Let my sister go, you over-grown tin can!" he cried. "That has to be The Blue Knight from the basement."

Jake scooped up the flashlight as fast as he could and jumped onto Gertrude's back. "Let's go, you guys," he shouted.

Mrs. Panosh leaped up as Rex poked his head out of Gertrude's feathers, terrified of what would happen next. A multicolored haze of smoke radiated from the spirits as they moved closer to Gertrude.

Just as the four suits seemed like they were about to grab them, Jake screamed to Gertrude, "Quick, Gerty, fly! Fly like the wind. Follow that suit of armor and knock down anything in your way!"

Gertrude bravely took flight, flapping her wings as wide and as strongly as she could. Sneezing and honking, she soared right over the helmets of the suits of armor, their feathers waving from the breeze of her flapping wings as she flew over them. With Jake guiding her every turn, she flew as fast as she could to catch up with Alexa and the armored monster. Gertrude flew to the left and then to the right, zigzagging down the treacherous dark tunnels. They could hear the other suits of armor chasing them from behind as they followed the echoes of Alexa's screams. Gertrude flew fearlessly in and out of every twist and turn.

"Rex—," Jake shouted as they flew around the walls of the maze, holding on tightly with every twist and turn Gertrude made. "Throw the ball of yarn at the Knights."

With Alexa's life in danger, Rex's cat courage was in full swing. He grabbed the gigantic ball of yarn from Gertrude's deep, white feathers and threw it with all his might towards the fast approaching Knights. Rex looked behind him to see if he had scored as Gertrude continued in hot pursuit of Alexa and her armor-plated kidnapper.

"Yes!" screamed Rex. The ball of yarn was a direct hit.

The huge ball of yarn quickly unraveled. As it spun around the legs of the four Knights of Lion Heart, they became twisted in Rex's rainbow web of yarn, collided into each other, and tumbled down to the ground.

"Where are we headed, Mrs. Panosh?" shouted Jake, as he rode Gertrude like a thoroughbred race horse.

"I think we're moving towards the back end of the kitchen's pantry, dear boy," she yelled through the dusty wind.

As Gertrude got closer and closer to Alexa and her steel kidnapper, Jake could see the light from his flashlight bouncing off the back of the suit of armor.

"Lexy," cried Jake, "throw me the backpack."

"Why?" she screamed.

"I don't think he wants you. I think he wants something in the backpack."

"You're too far away, Jake," she cried.

As the suit of armor came to a dead end, the wall opened up, and he carried Alexa, kicking and screaming, through to another secret passageway.

Gertrude was flying as fast as a rocket ship on its way to the moon. As she turned the corner, Jake could see no sign of Alexa but realized they were headed right into a dead end wall. Gertrude was sneezing so loudly she was unable to hear Jake tell her to slow down before they hit the wall. Jake, Rex, and Mrs. Panosh screamed at the top of their voices, afraid they were about to crash right into the stone wall. Just as they were about to hit, the wall opened up. Gertrude soared right through, colliding in the dark with Alexa and the suit of armor.

chapter eight
King Me

Just at that moment, the lights, which the storm had blown out, came back on. Instead of hitting the stone wall, they had all landed in sacks and sacks of vanilla baking powder stored in the kitchen pantry. Gertrude could not stop sneezing. All of them were covered in vanilla powder from head to toe.

Delbert, Mrs. Smythe, and The Duke of Snuffles, who had just arrived, went running to see what all the commotion was.

"My pantry! My pantry!" Mrs. Smythe cried out in disbelief. "What have you done to my pantry?"

They were all piled up, one on top of another, like a gigantic, vanilla ice cream cone.

"Inspector, is that you in there?" Delbert asked scratching his head.

"It sure is," Jake answered as he brushed the powder from his eyes.

"*It's going to take me a month to lick this powder off myself,*" complained Rex, licking his right paw to wash his face.

"Are you O.K., Lexy?" asked Jake.

"I think so!" Alexa said angrily as she unsuccessfully tried to grab her backpack from the mean suit of armor.

Gertrude let out another huge sneeze and a honk as she ruffled her feathers to shake off the vanilla powder.

"***Penny***, is that you in there, too?" asked Delbert.

"Yes, dear brother, it is I," answered Mrs. Panosh.

"***Brother!***" screamed Jake, Alexa, and Rex.

"Mrs. Panosh is your sister?" Jake asked Delbert.

"Why, yes, she is, Inspector. But I'm not exactly sure why you're here, Penny," he said as he looked at her with questioning eyes.

"I know exactly why she's here!" yelled Mrs. Smythe, waving a black frying pan like a major league baseball player about to hit a home run. "You came to ruin my cake, didn't you? Why, I bet you probably stole the bell so I couldn't even bake my cake. But even without time working, I managed to bake the best cake ever."

"I did no such thing, you horrible woman," yelled back Mrs. Panosh. "I had nothing to do with The Bell of Time missing. I came here to visit my brothers! Your awful cake is of no concern to me.

"By the way, how could you possibly bake a cake without time working? How would you know when it was done baking?" she asked, blowing vanilla powder into Mrs. Smythe's face.

"Jasper counts for her when she bakes," explained Alexa, still tugging her backpack from the suit of armor.

"How convenient for you," said Mrs. Panosh. "And where did you say you hid the bell, exactly?"

"How dare you!" screeched Mrs. Smythe, grabbing a

whisk out of her gadget drawer and waving it under Mrs. Panosh's nose. "I did not stop time! Why don't you go back to the zoo? I'll bet there's a monkey or two who need some mush to eat."

"Ladies, ladies, please. This is no way to solve this crime," said The Duke of Snuffles, trapped between them as they pushed and shoved him to get at each other.

"You're right, Duke," said Jake. "But figuring out what this gigantic, armor-plated tin can wants with my sister's backpack may be just the way to solve this crime."

The Duke and Delbert helped everyone up from the floor of the pantry and brought them into the kitchen. There they dusted themselves off so Gertrude could finally stop sneezing.

Delbert went to the broom closet to get a dust pan and a broom to clean up the powdery mess. Suddenly, Mrs. Smythe ran in front of him and screamed, "Stop! Stop! What do you think you're doing?"

"I'm getting a broom, dear lady!" Delbert exclaimed.

"This is my kitchen!" she yelled. "Stay out of my broom closet! I will get a vacuum cleaner later and clean up this filthy mess."

Delbert shuffled away, shocked at how rude she was. Jake thought it odd she wouldn't let Delbert near the broom closet.

"She's even grumpier than before!" whispered Rex.

"My detective skills are telling me she's hiding something in the closet," Jake whispered back to Rex.

Alexa still would not let go of her backpack as the suit dragged it and her across the red and black checkerboard

floor of the kitchen. "Let go of my backpack, you big bully!" she demanded, tugging and tugging on the pink and purple straps.

Jake went over to the vanilla-covered suit of armor and asked him, "You want something in the backpack, don't you?"

The suit nodded his tarnished, steel helmet up and down in the motion of yes.

"Well, we know it's not my can of tuna or my litter box, because they're not in there!" Rex smirked.

"I can't believe after all we've been through, you're still whining about that," scolded Jake, giving Rex the evil eye.

"Sorry!" Rex scowled, putting his powdery, white paws over his face in shame.

Alexa, still on the floor tugging away, pleaded, "Jake, make him let go."

Jake stood firmly in front of the mysterious suit of armor that was staring him down. They looked like two warriors about to do battle. The suit of armor moved two red checkerboard squares on the floor to the right, dragging Alexa, who still wouldn't let go of her Inspector Girl backpack. Jake then moved two black squares to the left following the knight in hot pursuit. They began to play a game of human checkers using the red and black square tile on the kitchen floor as a gigantic game board. There was only going to be one player Kinged. Jake knew he would be the last man standing.

"Everybody out of the way," announced Jake. *"He's— MINE!"*

Alexa finally let go of her backpack and stomped out of

the way in a huff.

The suit of armor moved two red squares back, and Jake went two black squares forward. The armor moved three reds to the left, and Jake moved three blacks to the right.

"Oh, no!" cried Alexa, "Jake is cornered by Mrs. Smythe's pot rack and the kitchen counter."

"Your move, **big guy,**" Jake smirked with a wink and a grin to his sister.

Just as the suit of armor jumped one red square to the left, Jake boldly leaped up onto a stool and ran across the kitchen counter. He grabbed onto the copper pot rack hanging from the ceiling and swung as hard as he could in mid-air, knocking the treacherous suit of armor to the floor.

"KING ME!!!!!!!!!!!!!!!!!!!!!!" Jake shouted as he jumped down from the pot rack.

Dazed, the suit of armor laid there on the red and black-tiled floor of the kitchen. Jake grabbed the backpack, unzipped it, and reached in, pulling out the black and white zebra-striped cashmere scarf.

chapter nine
A False Knight In Time

Jake dangled the scarf under the nose of the suit of armor. "Is this what you're looking for?" he questioned, dropping the scarf on the floor next to the bewildered knight. Jake dug deeper into the backpack and found the set of keys with the engraved 'S' on each one. He held out the keys as if he was about to hand them to the suit of armor. Just as the knight reached for them, Jake said, "Not so fast!" He pulled them back.

"My keys! My keys!" yelled The Duke of Snuffles. "I've been looking for them everywhere. I didn't know what happened to them. Where ever did you find them?"

"They were in the basement next to The Blue Knight," explained Jake. "So the 'S' stands for Snuffles, not suits of armor?"

"Why, yes," he said, "but I was never near the blue-feathered suit last night."

"Some time during the evening your keys were stolen by the culprit who took The Bell of Time," Jake said as he started to examine the mysterious suit of armor on the floor with his magnifying glass. "The criminal must have accidentally dropped them in the basement."

The Case Of Stolen Time

At that moment everyone was stunned. The four Knights of Lion Heart came stumbling though the secret opening in the pantry wall. They entered the kitchen dragging the rainbow trail of yarn from the ball Rex had thrown at them in the tunnel. They surrounded the downed, powder-covered suit of armor. The Yellow Knight aimed his cross bow at the fallen suit, while The Purple Knight raised his dagger, and The Red and Green Knights stood guard.

"How many keys are supposed to be on this key ring, Duke?" questioned Jake.

"Five, Inspector," answered The Duke of Snuffles.

"You know, my armored friend, the way these four other suits have surrounded you, a good detective would come to the conclusion they are a little mad at you," Jake said. He continued inspecting every inch of the armored suit. "Why, I'd bet my magnifying glass they weren't chasing us in the tunnel, after all. They were chasing you!"

Jake bent over to examine the foot of the suit but found no scratches on the armor's right foot, like the ones on the blue-feathered suit in the basement. He also noticed the suit of armor didn't have a blue feather on its helmet either. "It was dark down there, but I do remember a large scratch on the foot of the suit when I bent over to pick up the keys," he declared. "You also seem to be missing your blue feather. You're not The Blue Knight from the basement after all!"

From the backpack, Jake pulled the book from the library that The Green Knight had stabbed as a clue — *A False Knight in Time.* "Now I understand what this book means," he explained. "The spirit of The Green Knight was trying to tell us that there was a fake knight in a phony

79

suit running around the museum. It wasn't one of The Five Knights of Lion Heart, at all."

Looking down at the suit, surrounded by the Knights, Jake announced, "You're the false knight in time, an imposter!" Looking down at the false knight, he accused, "I now know who you are and who stole The Bell of Time!"

The kitchen was abuzz, wondering who Jake was about to unmask as the culprit.

"I know! I know!" shouted Alexa as she raised her hand waving it wildly, as if she were in school.

"*It was*—Miss Pumpernickel, in the garden, with the candlestick!"

They all gasped in disbelief.

"**NO, IT WASN'T!**" shouted Jake as he gave her an annoyed look.

"*Oh, I know! I know!*" shouted Rex as he raised his paw, shaking it wildly. "*It was General Ketchup, in the game room, with the dagger!*"

They all gasped again in disbelief.

Jake glared at Rex as if he was going to explode and sternly said, "**NO, IT WASN'T.** We are not playing a game of House Detective. Would you two let me finish?"

"Sorry!" said Rex and Alexa.

As Jake was arguing with Rex, Mrs. Panosh quietly slipped away from the group. She grabbed Mrs. Smythe's upside-down, down-side-up, pineapple cake off the counter and snuck it over to the mantel by Jasper without anyone noticing. She gave him a kiss hello and slid the cake right under Jasper's nose.

The Case Of Stolen Time

She then winked at Jasper and without a sound made her way back, unnoticed, into the group awaiting Jake's announcement of who stole The Bell of Time.

Jake pulled up the face shield on the helmet on the false knight and declared, "**_Lord Beasley_**, you are the culprit who stole The Bell of Time!"

chapter ten
The Perfect Crime

"Beasley, how could you?" scolded Delbert as he fidgeted with the clocks on his suspenders.

"I am innocent, I say, innocent!" cried Lord Beasley as he stood up.

"If you didn't do it, why did you grab my Inspector Girl backpack and carry me off, you big bully?" asked Alexa as she kicked his suit of armor.

"You grabbed the backpack so you could get rid of the clues we found throughout the museum," Jake said, grabbing the scarf off the floor.

"Clues, clues," he said, "what clues?"

"This is your scarf we found on the steps leading up to the clock tower," explained Jake. "You were wearing it last night and showed it to everyone at the party. Did you ever find your glasses, Lord Beasley?"

"Why, no. I went looking for them and was dragged into the tunnel by these crazy Knights. They have kept me prisoner ever since. I'm innocent," Lord Beasley cried. "I had nothing to do with the missing bell."

"You're a good liar, Lord Beasley, but you're no match for Inspector Jake Moustachio," declared Alexa as she pulled out the crushed glasses that Jake had stepped on in the tunnel. She pulled over a stool and stood on it, looked him in the face, and placed what was left of the glasses on his nose. Then Alexa stepped down and gave Lord Beasley's suit of armor another swift kick.

"I knew he was the culprit!" screamed Mrs. Smythe.

"She made me do it!" cried Beasley.

"I had nothing to do with it. Be quiet, you old fool. You'll ruin everything," she snapped back at him.

Jake signaled the spirits of the Red and Green Knights to guard Mrs. Smythe.

"How dare you, Inspector," she cried. "Delbert, please help me."

"Let the Inspector finish," he snapped angrily.

"Mrs. Smythe planned this all along so she could win the baking contest," said Jake. "But she couldn't pull off this caper alone. She needed help. That's where Lord Beasley came in. She knew that Lord Beasley wanted to be The Keeper of Time and possess the power to control all the clocks and time itself. If time was lost and then somehow found by Lord Beasley, who actually was hiding the bell all along, he would be a hero."

"And I would lose my job!" exclaimed Delbert, pacing back and forth across the checkerboard floor.

"Everyone knows that Rupert could never be the next time keeper with his bad eyesight," said Mrs. Panosh.

"*That would leave Lord Beasley wide open to take the job,*" said Rex.

"Controlling the clock and the bell would have given him enormous power and prestige," Delbert explained.

"Mrs. Smythe gave The Duke of Snuffles the lemon tart that she had added extra sour lemons to," said Jake.

"It was just enough to make him sick so she could get rid of him from the party early," said Alexa.

"Have you ever tasted such awful tarts!" exclaimed Mrs. Panosh.

"*I think I'm a little sick from the one that I ate,*" moaned Rex, rolling on the floor in fake pain.

"When she gave The Duke of Snuffles his coat, she snatched his keys from his coat pocket," revealed Jake. "She hid the keys in the drawer of vanilla baking powder in the back of the pantry."

"That's why they were covered with the vanilla powder when we found them in the basement," replied Alexa.

"Right!" continued Jake. "When all the guests from the party were about the leave, Lord Beasley pretended he had lost his glasses somewhere in the museum earlier."

"*That gave him an excuse to move around the museum without anyone being suspicious of him,*" added Rex.

"After hiding the keys, Mrs. Smythe's hands were covered in the vanilla powder when she handed Beasley his coat and scarf," declared Jake.

"That's why the scarf smelled like vanilla!" exclaimed Alexa.

"Lord Beasley went up the stairs to the clock tower to steal The Bell of Time, but dropped his scarf in front of the library door. Rupert found it later when he put his tray of food out for Mrs. Smythe to pick up," said Jake.

"Lord Beasley stole the bell," added Jake, "but he and Mrs. Smythe knew he would never make it out of the museum without getting caught."

"They must have planned to use the secret passageways and the tunnels to smuggle the bell out of the museum," said Alexa.

"Right," said Jake. "Lord Beasley made his way into the tunnel behind the picture of Lord Grimthorpe, just as we did. He then made his way to the pantry where he hid the bell in the same drawer of vanilla baking powder where The Duke of Snuffles' keys had been hidden earlier by Mrs. Smythe."

"That's why there was so much vanilla powder in the tunnels, causing Gertrude to sneeze and sneeze," said Mrs. Panosh.

"Right again," replied Jake. "He then went back into the tunnel to make his way out of the museum without anyone noticing."

"*But something went wrong!*" chimed in Rex.

"He dropped his glasses in the tunnel," explained Jake as he pointed to the broken pair of glasses dangling off the tip of Lord Beasley's nose.

"Without your glasses, Beasley," said Delbert, "you would never be able to find your way out of the secret mazes in the tunnels."

"Lord Beasley," said Jake, "you must have stumbled by accident upon that old suit of armor in the tunnels. Mrs. Panosh told us that during The Great War of Antwerp the army used the mazes to hide their spare armor from their enemies. By putting it on, you knew no one would discover it was you lurking about. Once out of the mazes, you could have walked right out of here disguised as one of The Knights of Lion Heart."

"That's right!" exclaimed Alexa. "But he got trapped in there like a mouse in a maze. The Knights of Lion Heart started chasing him, knowing he was the false knight."

"*I just love a good mouse chase!*" yelled Rex, fiddling with his new ball of yarn.

"Trapped behind the walls of the museum, you've been able to hear everything that has been going on with our investigation," accused Jake, facing Lord Beasley.

"That's why you grabbed me and my Inspector Girl backpack, you big bully," added Alexa as she gave him another kick in the suit. "You knew we put all of the clues in there. If you got my backpack, my brother would never be able to solve this crime."

"When Delbert realized time had stopped, he went running up to the clock tower," said Jake. "Jasper was taking a nippy nap, which gave Mrs. Smythe the perfect chance to grab the keys and The Bell of Time and make her way to the basement. There she hid the bell in the blue-feathered suit of armor."

"You must have had such a hard time opening up the helmet with the one key," he said to Mrs. Smythe, "that you didn't notice dropping the rest of The Duke of Snuffles' keys."

"That's why we found the keys in the basement near the foot of the suit of armor," said Alexa.

"Right you are, my clever sister! When the powdered keys hit the floor, the vanilla baking powder got all over the foot of The Blue Knight's armor."

"But why use the blue-feathered suit of armor as the hiding place?" asked Rex.

"I think I can answer that for you," said Snuffles on his way down to the basement to look for the blue-feathered suit of armor. "The suits were only going to be in the museum for a short period of time. Then they were going back to the five relatives of the Grimthorpe family. Lord Beasley's wife, Lady Beasley, is a distant cousin of Lord Grimthorpe."

"It all makes for a perfect crime!" declared Jake. "Lord Beasley and Mrs. Smythe knew that the blue-feathered suit containing the stolen Bell of Time would be carried right out of here and be delivered to the home of Lord and Lady Beasley. Lord Beasley planned to open up the suit eventually, find The Bell of Time, and become the hero."

"Delbert looks like he can't keep track of time and winds up losing his job. Lord Beasley, the hero, becomes The Keeper of Time."

"And Mrs. Smythe," continued Alexa, "being the only person able to bake a cake without using time, relying on Jasper's counting for her own personal clock, would be the only one able to bake a successful cake. That would assure her first place in the town's baking contest."

"A perfect crime!" exclaimed Rex.

"It would have been a perfect crime if you two nosey children and that whiny cat hadn't come through that darn magnifying glass!" screeched Mrs. Smythe.

The four spirits guarded Mrs. Smythe and Lord Beasley closely.

"We know who the culprits are," announced Jake. "We know why and how they stopped time. We also know The Bell of Time is inside the blue-feathered suit."

"All you have to do, Inspector," Delbert said, "is find the suit, and the missing key and time can be restored."

Just at that moment, The Duke of Snuffles came running up from the basement and shouted, "It's gone! The blue-feathered suit of armor is missing!"

Suddenly, Jake remembered Rupert telling him to ask the right questions to get the right answers. "Mrs. Smythe," he asked, "where is the blue-feathered suit of armor, now?"

"I have no idea," she answered, "and I wouldn't help you even if I knew."

Out of the corner of his eye, Jake saw the hazy, blue smoke of the spirit of The Blue Knight flying near Mrs. Smythe's broom closet. He knew, by the way she answered his question, that she was lying. While they had been in The Library of Time, she must have taken the blue-feathered suit and hidden it in such a good hiding place no one would ever find it. He remembered how upset she was when Delbert went to the broom closet for a broom.

"I think I should get a broom to clean up this vanilla powder," Jake announced as he walked closer and closer to the broom closet. "We should pick up some of this powder; you never know when you may need more vanilla to bake another cake."

Mrs. Smythe finally noticed the missing cake that Mrs. Panosh had snuck over to Jasper.

The Case Of Stolen Time

"My cake!" screamed Mrs. Smythe. "My cake! Where is my upside-down, down-side-up, pineapple cake?"

They all turned around and gasped to see that Jasper was eating the cake, pineapples and all.

chapter eleven
Just Desserts

Mrs. Smythe became enraged and darted away from the suits that were guarding her. She ran yelling and screaming towards Jasper. "My cake! My beautiful cake! What do you think you're doing, you mangy, smelly moose? Stop eating my cake."

Jasper was chomping away at the upside-down, down-side-up, pineapple cake, paying no attention to Mrs. Smythe's hysteria and her wild and crazy ranting.

"You've ruined everything, you hairy beast!" she screamed. "Now I won't have anything to enter into the contest, just like last year."

She turned towards Mrs. Panosh and began her tirade, "You did this! You were the one last year who put my cake on the mantel, so Jasper would eat it. You've been jealous of my baking for years. Now I'm ruined."

Mrs. Panosh walked right up to Mrs. Smythe with a satisfied grin on her face. "You can always cook mush at the zoo, my dear," Mrs. Panosh smirked.

At that moment, Jasper's eyes started bulging out of his head, and he made horrible noises as he began to choke on a piece of pineapple.

"Serves you right," Mrs. Smythe scolded as Jasper tried to swallow the pineapple with no luck. "I've had to put up with your antics in this kitchen long enough. Now you will get your just desserts. Go ahead, **Choke on it, you hairy beast! Choke on it!**" Mrs. Smythe yelled as her face turned redder than her red uniform.

Jasper continued to try to clear his throat, when Mrs. Smythe grabbed a rolling pin. She swung it in the air in Jasper's direction. Everyone ducked as she moved closer and closer to the mantel. She was in a wild rage, swirling the pin as she moved.

"That's some fur ball he's about to throw up!" Rex said, covering his eyes.

"It looks like he's going to blow!" shouted Jake as he and everyone else, including the suits of armor, took ten steps back to avoid getting hit.

In one gigantic burst, Jasper spit out the entire upside-down, down-side-up, pineapple cake all over Mrs. Smythe. She was covered with it from head to toe.

"It looks like dessert is on you, my dear," laughed Mrs. Panosh. "Are you alright Jasper? Was the cake too awful to eat?" she asked as she wiped his snout with her pink, linen handkerchief.

"I was choking on something sharp," he said adoringly as he gave her a snuggle and a pineappley kiss.

Jake grabbed the magnifying glass from his back pocket and searched the cake-covered floor for any signs of a sharp object. "I got it!" he yelled in excitement. "I got it!" Jake bent over and picked up The Duke of Snuffles' missing fifth key.

Everyone's mouths dropped open as Jake cleaned the

cake off of the key. "Very clever, Mrs. Smythe," noted Jake, "hiding the key in the drawer of vanilla baking powder and then baking it into the cake where no one would ever find it."

"But my brother is more clever than that!" exclaimed Alexa.

"Well, I better go get that broom from the closet and clean up this mess," said Jake as he made his way to the broom closet door with the spirit of The Blue Knight circling around his head.

"**NOOOOOOOOOO!**" cried Mrs. Smythe as the Red and Green Knights drew their swords preventing her from stopping Jake.

"*Your goose is cooked now, Mrs. Smythe,*" said Rex.

"**HONK! HONK!**" cried Gertrude.

"*Sorry, Gerty,*" said Rex.

Jake tried to open up the broom closet door, but it was stuck. He pulled and pulled with no luck. Alexa ran up behind him quickly and pulled on him, like a piece of rope in a tug of war. Jake held on tightly to the door knob, but they could not budge the door open.

"*What is it with door knobs in this place? They either fall off or won't open,*" Rex said as he joined in the tug of war.

They looked like a human train as Mrs. Panosh, Snuffles, and Gertrude joined them in pulling the door. But still the door stuck. Finally, Delbert joined the back of the line, like a caboose, and helped give one last hard tug. As the door finally flew open, they all fell backwards on top of each other like bowling pins being knocked down by a direct hit.

As they staggered to their feet, there it was—the blue-feathered suit of armor with the vanilla baking powder still on its foot and a large scratch on the armor.

"You did it, Jake!" cried Alexa.

"Oh, yes, Inspector, you did it!" congratulated Delbert.

"Since Mrs. Smythe is guilty, I'm going to get to come home," said Mrs. Panosh, hugging Gertrude.

"Honk!" said Gertrude.

"Don't worry, Gerty, you can come live here, too!"

"Come on, let's wrap this crime up. I'm going to need my litter box any minute!" complained Rex.

"We did it!" Jake said, smiling from ear to ear.

The spirit of the Blue Knight swirled around, happy to have come home to his old, rusty suit of armor. After he entered through the helmet, he came walking out of the closet and joined the other four knights. Everyone was trembling in anticipation of what they were about to find in the helmet. Jake took the fifth and final key, reached up to the back of the helmet, and gave the key a turn.

They all held their breath as the back of the helmet opened. Jake reached inside and pulled out The Bell of Time. As Delbert had said, it was no bigger than a walnut, but it was magnificent. A brilliant light reflected from the bright gold metal the bell was made of.

The spirits of The Knights of Lion Heart went flying out of their suits of armor and danced together in a dazzling explosion of color throughout the kitchen.

Jake closed his eyes as he held the precious Bell of

Time. He trembled as he felt the power of the bell enter him. With his eyes shut tight, Jake could feel the passage of time and events throughout his life. He got to revisit some of the happiest moments of his past eleven years as they flashed before him: his first birthday party when he stuck his lollypop in his birthday cake, scoring the winning soccer goal while his dad coached, his grandpa teaching him to swim at the beach. Jake smiled happily as the most wonderful moments of his life played in his mind like a movie, ending right back at this exact moment in time.

"That's awesome!" he said as he handed the bell to Alexa.

Alexa held the bell ever so cautiously. It was as if a newborn kitten was sleeping in her hand. "I can feel and see all my birthdays, play dates, and Mommy braiding my hair," she said. "It's like a video all about me!"

She next placed The Bell of Time into Rex's paws. He held it as the glow radiated from the gold, illuminating his whiskers. He closed his big golden eyes and saw the most wonderful moments from his life: his mommy and daddy, all ten of his brothers and sisters, and the day he was adopted by the Moustachios. He purred as a tear dropped from the corner of his eye.

Rex passed The Bell of Time back to Jake who carefully handed it off to Delbert. "I believe this belongs to you," he said.

The Case Of Stolen Time

"Time belongs to no one Inspector, and yet, it belongs to everyone," said Delbert. "It is just mine to watch over till the next timekeeper takes my place. The three of you are now members of a very special group who have had the privilege to feel the power and majesty of time. Remember that feeling and let it carry you through the rest of your lives."

"We will!" they all shouted gratefully. "We will!"

chapter twelve
Beware Of The Baron

Delbert ran up to the clock tower and found the door knob to open the door. He placed The Bell of Time into the center of The Great Clock. At that moment, all the clocks that could be seen and heard started to turn, crank, and ring once again. As Delbert adjusted the big hand on The Great Clock ever-so-gently, all time fell back into place.

Delbert had a big smile on his face as he turned to leave the tower. As he made his way to the door, he slid on a bunch of glow sticks and went crashing onto the floor. He stood up and looked around the tower at the many glow sticks scattered about the floor, laughing himself silly as he gathered them all up. He walked down the steps back to the kitchen, still amused as he rejoined the others.

Handing Alexa the sticks, he said, "I believe these belong to you, little lady." Alexa gathered up the glow sticks and placed them into her Inspector Girl backpack.

Jake turned towards the two culprits he had just caught and asked, "What do we do about these two?"

The five spirits of The Knights of Lion Heart re-entered their suits of armor and surrounded Mrs. Smythe and Lord Beasley.

"Oh, don't worry, Inspector," said Snuffles. "The knights and I will take care of Mrs. Smythe and Lord Beasley until the police arrive."

"I must run up to the library and tell Rupert the good news," said Mrs. Panosh, putting on an apron decorated with an embroidered clock design.

"*Won't he be upset he won't get to be the new Keeper of Time?*" asked Rex.

"Oh, he'll be so excited to have his sister back, baking away here at the museum, he'll forget all about that!" replied Mrs. Panosh. "Come, Gerty."

Before Mrs. Panosh left to make her way up to the library, she gave Jake and Alexa a big kiss on the forehead and thanked them for their help. "I had a wonderful misadventure with you three," she said. "We'll have to do it again sometime. Gertrude, give Rex a kiss goodbye!"

Rex's eyeballs nearly flew out of his little, furry head when Gertrude picked him up and gave him the wettest duck kiss he'd ever gotten.

"Honk! Honk!" she cried as they made their way up to the library.

"*Yuck!*" he moaned. "*That overgrown duck slobbered all over me and nearly sucked all my fur right off!*"

"For the last time," Jake said, "she's a goose, not a duck!"

"Thank you, Inspector," Delbert said. "Your grandfather would be proud of you. Proud of all of you!"

"You knew Grandpa?" questioned Alexa as she pulled a piece of rainbow yarn from the back of The Purple Knight and made a colorful ponytail tie for her hair.

"Oh, yes. Your grandfather was the greatest detective there ever was. Why, he and that magnifying glass got into a lot of misadventures of their own when he was younger. It was given to him by his grandfather."

Delbert continued, "The magnifying glass has quite a history to it. Your great-great-grandfather, Inspector Jake Moustachio, who you are named after, was given the magnifying glass from a famous English detective in the nineteenth century with the initials 'S. H.' "

"You mean Sher—," said Jake.

"Don't say his name!" interrupted Delbert. "His identity must never be revealed. Your great-great-grandfather and this famous detective were working on a case together in Ireland when they stumbled upon two magnifying glasses in a cave just outside the town of Dublin. The magnifying glasses turned out to be part of an ancient treasure Leprechauns had hidden in many caves throughout all of Ireland.

"Knowing how dangerous it would be for one person to possess the powers of both magnifying glasses, they decided each would take one. Inspector Moustachio kept one in his possession and went back to America, and the other went back to England with 'S. H.' "

"Where is the other one now?" asked Alexa inquisitively.

"Well, history has it that the magnifying glass that went to England was supposedly stolen by the evil Baron Von Snodgrass, who, after stealing the magnifying glass, jumped into it and vanished, never to be seen or heard from again.

"Legend also has it that the one who has the purest of thoughts and heart and possesses both magnifying glasses will be able to solve all the mysteries of the universe.

"You must be very careful every time you jump through the magnifying glass," warned Delbert. "Evil lurks quietly in some places behind the glass. Baron Von Snodgrass and his henchmen will stop at nothing to get the other magnifying glass. Word will soon spread that you, Inspector Jake Moustachio, saved time. You will be called again from many sources for your help.

"I fear that if Baron Von Snodgrass finds out that you now possess the other magnifying glass, he may, after all this time, come out of hiding looking for you," shuddered Delbert.

"Don't worry, Delbert. I can handle him," boasted Jake.

"Me, too!" said Alexa.

"*Are you two crazy?*" exclaimed Rex. "*You want to mess with an evil Baron? We need to give that magnifying glass back to your grandma the minute we get home.*"

"No way," shouted Jake. "The magnifying glass is my birthday present. You never give back a present."

"**Unless** you get two of the same things," said Alexa. "Once I got two Bridgette U.S.A. dolls. Mommy and I exchanged one for a Victoria doll. Then and only then is it O.K. to return a birthday present."

"This is my magnifying glass, and no one, not even Baron Von Snodgrass, is going to take it from me!" declared Jake.

Delbert pulled a clock off of his suspenders and handed it to Jake to remember him by. "Anytime you need me," said Delbert, "just wind up the clock and look through the magnifying glass, and you will find me."

"Oh, no!" cried Alexa, looking at the clock. "Grandma must be so worried about us. I'm sure she's finished her crossword puzzle by now and is frantically searching for us."

"Don't worry, little lady," explained Delbert. "Every time you go back through the magnifying glass, you will arrive exactly at the same time you left. It's as if you've never been gone! After all, I should know. I am The Keeper of Time!"

Alexa gathered up her Inspector Girl backpack as Jake took out the magnifying glass from his back pocket.

"You guys ready to go home?" he asked.

"*My litter box awaits me!*" exclaimed Rex happily.

"Bye, Jasper," said Alexa.

"Bye, Inspector, Alexa, and Rex," he said.

"You know," said Alexa with a crinkle in her forehead, "I think I need a name."

"What name?" asked Jake. "You have a name."

"I need a detective name!" she exclaimed.

"That's stupid!" Jake protested.

"Why do you get to have a name? I've heard nothing but Inspector this, Inspector that, all through this misadventure. I helped just as much. I want a name. I'm going to call myself—**Inspector Girl!**"

"Inspector Girl," he moaned.

"That's right—**Inspector Girl**," she yelled. "I love it! It matches my backpack and my personality!"

"*Well, if you both get names, I want one, too!*" shouted Rex.

"Oh, brother, not you, too," said Jake.

"*I'm going to call myself by my full name, Rexal*

Moustachio, Critter Detective."

"You must be kidding me," laughed Jake.

"*I can see it now. If your dog lost his bone or your squirrel can't find his nuts, call Rexal Moustachio, Critter Detective. If your critter's in trouble, I'm your pussy cat!*"

"I think that lemon tart and tuna affected your brain, you crazy fur ball," Jake said.

Delbert instructed Jake to read the words on the magnifying glass while thinking of where he wanted to go. Jake and Alexa read the words out loud as they thought of the attic back home.

**"*Through the magnifying glass you will see,
the many misadventures that can be.*"**

Jake looked once again into the magnifying glass and, to his amazement, saw his attic.

As before, the magnifying glass began to shake in Jake's hand. It fell to the ground as a huge flash of light bolted out of it and it grew larger and larger. An enormous gust of wind started to blow and twirl from the rim of the glass, filling up the kitchen like a small tornado.

"It's time to jump, Inspector," yelled Delbert through the vortex of wind.

"Jump in my backpack, Rex," instructed Alexa.

"*No way!*" yelled back Rex. "*I'm surfing this wave SOLO!*

"*Oh, and just in case I can't speak to you guys when we get home, remember, it's one meow for yes and two meows for no! Also remind your mother I hate that new cat litter; it smells like roses. And that shrimp surprise gives me gas. Tell the house keeper to stop sucking up my tail when she cleans under the beds. I also like a little tummy rub, now and then."*

"Jump already!" yelled Jake. "Jump!"

"Alright, I'm going. I'm going," Rex said. *"But just one more thing."*

"Oh, brother!" exclaimed Jake.

"You guys are the best brother and sister a pussy cat could ever want! I love you guys! Thanks for letting me tag along."

With that said, Rex made a flying leap into the magnifying glass, shouting *"My litter box awaits"* as he slid towards home.

Jake grabbed onto Alexa's hand.

"I'm a little scared," she cried, clutching his hand.

"I'd never let anything bad happen to you," he promised. "On three. **ONE—TWO—THREE!**"

"By the way, Delbert, how did you find me?" Jake asked as they leaped into the magnifying glass.

"Why everyone knows how to find The Great Inspector Moustachio!" he shouted through the wind. ***"I just called your receptionist!"***

Once again, they slid down the gigantic, seemingly-endless slide, twisting and turning inside the magnifying glass. They slid faster and faster with every bend on their way home as sparkles of color and flashing stars flew past them like fireworks on the Fourth of July.

"Ahhhhh!" screamed the children with wide smiles, this time laughing all the way.

"Goodbye, Inspector!" yelled Delbert. "Thank you, Alexa. I mean Inspector Girl!"

"See ya, Delbert," they shouted back.

chapter
thirteen
Bedtime

Rex came flying out of the magnifying glass into the
attic. He went crashing into an old box of stuffed animals,
sliding across the Christmas tinsel, which was still scattered
across the attic floor. A flash of light exploded into the room
as Alexa and Jake came tumbling through.

"You guys O.K.?" asked Jake.

"*Meow*," said Rex as he burst through the door, running
down the steps to his litter box.

"Well, I guess he had to go!" Alexa giggled.

Jake and Alexa looked curiously at the magnifying glass.
It was still enlarged, with the wind blowing through it as if
something was about to happen. Jake and Alexa stood back,
clinging to each other in the vortex of wind.

"Oh, no, Jake!" cried Alexa. "What if Baron Von
Snodgrass has come out of hiding and is coming through
the magnifying glass after us?"

Their eyes got larger and larger as another bolt of light
exploded from the glass. Out flew a small, blue box with
a large red and black checkered ribbon. Jake and Alexa
sighed in relief; it wasn't the Baron Von Snodgrass. Then
they giggled in anticipation of what was inside the box.

As Alexa approached the box, the magnifying glass shrunk to its normal size. Jake picked it up and once again placed it in his back pocket.

"What do you suppose is in the box?" asked Alexa.

"There's only one way to find out," said Jake. "Let's open it up!"

They quickly unwrapped the box to find a booklet of five gift certificates from The Library of Time, made out to Jake, Alexa, and Rex Moustachio.

A note was enclosed that read:

In case you need a little extra TIME in future adventures, just tear off one certificate and throw it into the wind. Good to stop TIME for one minute. Use them wisely.

Fondly, Rupert.

P.S. When you're finished reading the book, A False Knight in Time, please return it to the library!

"Lexy!" shouted Jake. "Did you keep that book?"

"I want Daddy to read it to me at bedtime," she said, raising her eyebrows. "It looks mysterious."

"And how were you planning to explain where you got it from?" he said with a wrinkle in his nose.

"Well! I didn't really think about that!" she explained. "You know, I'm only eight years old!"

Jake and Alexa heard Grandma's foot steps in the hallway. They quickly hid the gift certificates in the backpack.

"I'm almost done with my crossword puzzle," she said to them as she stumbled up the steps, her hair pins falling everywhere. "I just was stuck on one four letter word ending in 'E' for the measuring and passing of events."

Jake and Alexa looked at each other and smiled as they both screamed from the attic, *"TIME!"*

"That's right! You two are just too smart for your own good," she said, pulling a pencil out of her crazy hair as she wrote the last word to complete the crossword puzzle.

"Finished!" Grandma exclaimed. "And it's time to get ready for bed."

"O.K., Grandma, we're coming," they called, running down the attic stairs.

"My goodness, you two," she said. "You're covered head to toe with white dust from that filthy attic. You must have had quite an adventure up there!"

Jake and Alexa just stood there giggling, still covered in vanilla baking powder.

"Scoot into the bathroom, both of you, and I'll help you wash that off," said Grandma.

Jake and Alexa got washed up, and Grandma tucked them each into bed with a sweet kiss to both their cheeks.

Alexa was all snuggled in her purple satin U.S.A. Girl pajamas with her Inspector Girl backpack hanging from the corner of her white princess bed. Rex was there, too, curled up all warm and cozy on his favorite checkered blanket, still licking the vanilla powder from his fur.

Jake smiled as he lay in his blue race car bed.

A spark of light from his night light bounced off the magnifying glass as he twirled it in the palm of his hand.

He thought to himself about his Grandpa, Delbert, The Knights of Lion Heart, and The Bell of Time. He thought about the wonderful world he'd gotten to see, and he went to sleep dreaming of the many misadventures that were yet to be!

The End?

The Misadventures have just begun!

The mysteries of the magnifying glass become clearer to our young unsuspecting hero, Jake Moustachio, as he is drawn into a wild western world of deception. An ancient Indian burial ground awaits him, his sister Alexa, their crazy cat Rex and some uninvited dastardly guests on the other side of his Grandpa's mystical magnifying glass. Big Daddy, the biggest cow rancher there ever was and will ever be, calls upon Jake to find his kidnapped cows and a treasure map to the Indian burial ground that is hidden on one of the cows. Lurking behind every twist and turn is the evil Baron Von Snodgrass who will stop at nothing to steal the magnifying glass and seek his revenge on young Moustachio. There is only one guy who can find that treasure map and save the kidnapped cows from their imminent doom. Inspector Moustachio is his name and solving mysterious crimes is his specialty!

Join Inspector Jake Moustachio, his sister Alexa (*a.k.a. Inspector Girl*), and their crazy cat Rex in their next thrilling misadventure...

THE MYSTERY AT COMANCHE CANYON

about the author

Wayne Madsen is a dad from New Jersey. In 2007, he was nationally recognized as a **Reading is Fundamental (RIF)** booklist pick author for the first book in *The Misadventures of Inspector Moustachio* series.

Book one, ***The Case of Stolen Time***, book two, ***The Mystery of Comanche Canyon***, and book three, ***The Curse of Shipwreck Bottom***, have become must-reads on school and library reading lists.

The Misadventures of Inspector Moustachio series is also a celebrated winner of the distinguished **iParenting Media Award**, a Disney Interactive Group Media Property.

Wayne's inspiration for writing comes from the real-life antics and misadventures of his children, Jake and Alexa. Adding in the escapades of the Madsen's crazy pets, Wayne has created an amazing universe of unforgettable characters who have become favorites on family bookshelves everywhere.

Wayne has just completed the fourth book in *The Misadventures of Inspector Moustachio* series, ***The Secret of the Pharaoh's Feline***. He is currently working on book five, ***The Mishap with the Mad Scientist***.

IF YOU ENJOYED

The Case Of
Stolen Time

BE SURE TO READ

BOOKTWO
The Mystery at Comanche Canyon
ISBN 9780979087882

BOOK THREE
The Curse of Shipwreck Bottom
ISBN 9780979757228

AND DISCOVER THE REST
OF THE MISADVENTURES!

Look for
The Misadventures of Inspector Moustachio
series at your local bookstores and libraries, or order online.

Published By

Community PRESS

239 Windbrooke Lane, Virginia Beach VA 23462

Read What Educators Are Saying About

The Misadventures Of
Inspector Moustachio!

"Once you start reading this terrific book, you can't put it down! What a treasure for parents who want their children to enjoy reading."

JOYCE CARUSI
NJ Plus Reading Editor / Educational Publishing
14 year Director, Sylvan Learning Center

"A riveting tale of adventure and suspense! Let Jake and Alexa lead you to the culprit. A must read for all ages."

MICHELLE BARSHAY
3rd Grade Teacher / BA / MA
Curriculum & Instruction

"Thank you for creating a story that combines adventure and humor. I look forward to making this series a part of my classroom library."

JUDY REYNOLDS
1st Grade Teacher / BA / MA Reading
Specialist / Adjunct Professor, NJCU

"A desire to savor the moment gradually emerges as each page turns. Bursts of color, expressive language, the whimsical array of characters, and compelling storyline sprinkle the pages of this book craftily creating a fun-filled adventure."

PAMELA JOYCE, Ph.D
Reading Specialist
Urban Education Consultant

LaVergne, TN USA
27 November 2010
206463LV00006B/23/P